The Devil Catches Butterflies

Reese T. Lightfoot

NIGHT SCRIPT MEDIA

Night Script Media—Astoria, NY
ISBN: 979-8-218-36701-5
Library of Congress Control Number: 2024903401
Title: *The Devil Catches Butterflies*
Author: Reese T. Lightfoot
Digital distribution | 2024
Paperback | 2024

You may not control all the events that happen to you, but you can decide not to be reduced by them.

—*Maya Angelou*

Chapter One
The Monarch

For the longest time, the view of adult life seemed like an ageless chore, annoyingly contradicting every candle blown out year after year before indulging in a piece of cake. Unfortunately, this would more than likely result in questioning the Ikea scale in my bathroom. Each day, constantly seeking perfection, profits, and approval from a cast of characters that have no leading role in the movie of my life but sure as hell act as a director. My days and nights were often confined to four office walls or locked away in a small one-bedroom apartment. All while listening to the sounds of urban life, I read and corrected the endless dribble of horrible manuscripts that infiltrated my email like an unwanted parasite.

Who doesn't enjoy polishing hot garbage into manifestos, all to please the egos of the slightly misogynist, so-called creators in the heart of the big city? But hey, this is what I dreamt about as a teenage girl way back when, right? Living the life of Carrie Bradshaw, chatting it up with friends over brawny drinks, nibbling on overpriced New York City fare. Friends, influence, and money. That, plus my own literary works, just waiting to be viewed on the world's stage. But please excuse my rant. Let me introduce myself.

My name is Phoebe Graham. Probably the most famous nobody you'd ever heard of. Odds are, if you've ever peeled open a best-seller book to enjoy with a full glass of Chenin Blanc, I edited said work and probably contributed a batch of august ideas. However, make no mistake, even in the new progressive world of LGBTQI, BLM, and Feminism, having lady parts is still an occupational setback slash hazard. Especially when you work for a circular framed-glasses-wearing, egotistical, narcissistic, stupid hipster, mustache-having, tweed jacket-wearing ass: Sean V. Trembly. Unfortunately, Mr. Trembly just so happens to be on the New York Times best-seller list. His spicy works about improving your love life or romance novels where the Channing Tatum rip-off always gets the girl almost always managed to gobble up rave reviews and plenty of publicity. This guy's ego is so big that I don't have the slightest idea of how his head even fits in his stupid little turtle neck.

But how could I ever tell him that? Instead, as his underlings, we kindly grovel like Oliver Twist and accept the unfair wage that is given. But this was all about to change in a bizarre way.

"Phoebe, Phoebe!" A bassy voice shouted from behind the 45-degree crack of my office door.

It was Garrett Miller. Garrett was an older gentleman in the office. He sported a bushy gray beard, thick caterpillar-like eyebrows, and a polished-to-perfection bald head. Garrett was the Senior Copy Editor here at Monarch Publishing. If the other males here at Monarch were haunting the company with red-blooded energy, Garrett was lit sage, refreshing and cleansing.

"Oh hey, Garrett, I didn't hear you standing there for the last five minutes," removing the lone ear-bud from my sweaty ear canal with a smile.

"Just so you're aware, I had a chance to speak with Chris upstairs, and it seems that Trembly just submitted a new manuscript. Which, as you know, means more late nights and all hands on deck."

"No, not another one! Garrett, seriously!" slamming my head gently to my desk. *"I do have a smidge of a life, ya know. Just a smidge."*

Garrett chuckled a smile from beneath his bristly beard.

"Kid, I didn't get a life until I was well into my forties. No cap, isn't that what the youth say?"

Laughing as he crept away, leaving me screaming into the laminate of my cheap desk. Becoming a writer would be a dream come true, and deep in my gut, in some twisted way, being Trembly's lackey would help me reach that goal. Fate can be a real…well, for lack of better words, difficult person to work with. It was game on for the next two weeks: long meetings in the morning, brutal Zoom calls in the afternoon, and two or three energy drinks in the evening to get through the late office hours editing.

Monarch Publishing was located in SoHo, but my little slice of the apple pie was located in a touristy, upbeat part of Midtown. Every night this week, elevator car Number 8 was the first step to a New York winter's commute home, riding ten floors down, jogging to the D train, and cruising like a rickety bullet to my stop. It's only about a 20-minute ride, but that 20 minutes is my 20 minutes. Outside of this snappy business casual attire and deep in the depths of my fancy high-end messenger bag existed my guilty pleasure…comic books and tonight's comic of choice: The X-men. As the train gained speed and clickety-clack along the sparky metal rails, I dove deeper and deeper into my comic. Yet something seemed off. My senses could feel someone glaring at me, even through the sea of people inside the packed car.

Furtively poking my eyes above the top of my page, a young man was spotted making his best attempt to seem as if he wasn't staring in my direction. He had Twix-colored hair and deep brown eyes and was accompanied by the high-end fashion taste of many other New Yorkers in the SOHO area. Seriously, those loafers he's wearing had to be just north of 1000 dollars. Also, I'm not a watch aficionado, but in this city, you know a Breitling when you see it. Nevertheless, this was my stop, and it was time to get back to the grind.

The next day in the office consisted of more of the same news release hustle and bustle, but dare I say it, it was going smoothly. That was until Amber Lynn and Peyton Madison showed up, casually known around the office as… *"The Terror Twins."* You see, the Terror Twins came from money, like old waspy money, like leaving Jack in the water. I'm more important, so there is no space for you on this door, money. Amber Lynn, who just happened to be Trembly's friend slash agent, and Peyton, the designated family screw-up turned investor. With these two in the building, what could possibly go wrong? My phone began ringing as if the karma gods were sitting on my disheveled desk. It was Garrett. A dry gulp slid down the back of my windpipe, fixating on my screen's shaking green phone icon.

"Hey Garrett, what can I do ya for?"

"Hey, Phoebe just got word from Chris upstairs. The umm Twins called a meeting. The game's afoot, kiddo."

"Click."

Gathering up my edits thus far, the funeral march to the elevator began. Standing within the shiny rectangular box with craggy geometric carpeting, I couldn't help but watch each number light up on the indicator. Every ding lined up with every gas bubble popping within my stomach. Walking through those silver doors, passing glass office after office, this meeting began to seem more and more like a firing squad. All that was missing at this point was a bandana and a lit cigarette. Then it happened, that cringy British voice.

"Oh, and who is this, Chris?" said Amber Lynn in an elitist tone.

"Oh, my name is Phoebe Graham, we've actually met be…."

"I believe I said…Chris." Amber Lynn's polished red index finger came to a point.

Wow, talk about ridiculing. On that note, my place was made known. I clutched my laptop close to my chest and took a seat.

"This is Phoebe Graham. Amber Lynn, she is one of the members of Garrett's team who assists with the editing process of Trembly's newest piece."

Chris always had a passion for dropping the hammer on us, so it was actually quite refreshing seeing this lesser Matt Smith look-a-like kowtow to his slithery overlords.

"Speaking of! How close are we to completion with that, and have we decided on cover art? You know my dearest Sean is very busy, and we have VIPs that are waiting for products…Along with a slew of T.V. and radio interviews."

"Look, Chris!" It seemed the other twin was finally ready to chime in, stripping his face away from his phone.

"We don't have time for this," snapped Peyton. *"We have two other up-and-coming best-seller authors to publish, as well as a big streaming production coming for one of Sean's previous works! Just get this done!"*

"And when he says done, he means a fully edited manuscript by Friday morning," chimed Amber Lynn.

"Absolutely, Amber Lynn. *All resources will now be put forth as this is a top priority. We have yet to let down Mr. Trembly here at Monarch, and we certainly don't plan to do so now!"*

Yuck, look at Chris, rubbing his hands together like some sort of fly. What a suck-up.

"Well, Garrett, Chop Chop!" clapped Chris.

My pace slowed to match Garrett's, both of us silent as we walked down the hall. We made our way into the elevator side by side, only to turn our backs and watch the silver doors slide to a slam.

"Friday! Friday Garrett, is she insane? This is a 600-page novel! Not to mention, it's a total train

wreck. Who writes a tell-all memoir that tells absolutely nothing? No intimacy, no reveals, or saucy notes? It's as bland as white people's potato salad!"

Garrett pressed his thumb against his lips. *"Look, Phoebe, you know that I more than agree with you, but…"* paused Garrett.

"But what?"

"Well…can you keep a secret?"

"Of course."

"One of my contacts managed to get me a meeting with a House based out of the UK. If we can produce the numbers on this book, they're looking to move me into a Contract Manager role, and I'm bringing you on board."

My eyes instantly begin to puddle. Garrett's words stopped my mind clean in its tracks.

"Look, Phoebe, you've got talent; that much is clear. We all see it, Chris, for God's sake, sees it, and you know it. All that's needed from you is the grit and grind. If this works out, kid, we can get you the exposure you need and deserve."

Speechless and needless to say, convinced, he had my vote of confidence. The elevator reached Garrett's floor. He casually stepped out, giving me a dad-like thumb before disappearing into a thin black line. For the remainder of the evening, I hacked away at Trembly's memoir, stomaching the constant flow of midden infesting my laptop screen. Yet, this energy was different. My mind was stuck on Garrett's words. Being an editorial assistant isn't exactly horrible, but to have my writing career pushed would be huge! But it's that time again, and my little nook in Midtown is calling my name. Proceeding with my usual train ritual, I couldn't help but notice that the 1000-dollar loafer guy was back on the train. Not sure what's gotten into me, my eyes were unable to look away from him. He's not even my type. Then again, it's been a while, and focusing on tonight's comic choice was even becoming difficult.

"God Loves Man Kills," interrupted a voice.

Wha… What, is the Loafer guy talking to me? Pretending to raise my eyes from the middle of the page, we made contact.

"Excuse me," I replied with fake puzzlement.

"God Loves Man Kills, the X-Men comic that you're reading. It's one of my favorites."

Wow, shocking, didn't expect a guy that looked like him to know his comics?

"Um, yeah, definitely one of Chris Claremont's best works,"

"You're on this train a lot. I'm Alvin, and you are…?" He fired, extending his cold leather-gloved hand. Speechless, blinking like some odd praying mantis, my name managed to come out of my mouth.

"Phoebe."

"Well, Phoebe, it's always a pleasure to meet a fellow comic book nerd. Guess I'll catch you next time."

And just like that, Alvin disappeared into the shuffle of New Yorkers on the platform, like an Ace in a dealer's deck.

That night in my apartment, my mind couldn't stop thinking about my interaction with Alvin. I guess I really did judge a book by its cover. A rather fitting metaphor for an editorial assistant. Ugh, I'm doing it again…. time to get back on task. There's plenty of work to be done. Now is not the time for swooning. If we don't get this right, the Terror Twins will make Garrett's life, as well as mine, a nightmare. Easier said than done because the next day at work, my game was way off!

All I could think about was Alvin. Needless to say, I'm not the type of girl that often gets a lot of attention, but at least my cat, Sith, loves me. As the work day came to a close, I found myself fumbling along more than ever, so much so that I left my laptop at my desk by accident. Then, my phone, which caused me to miss the elevator by a fraction of a second… which means odds are I'll miss the train…Great! But truthfully, this was never about catching the train on time. Deep down inside, this was about a geeky woman meeting a guy that she's into and watching that very moment about to crumble. As soon as the elevator doors opened, I dashed through Monarchs' lobby like a cheetah wearing a jetpack. I quickly ran into the subway, skipping steps along the way, which was not an easy feat in the three-inch booties on my feet.

"Crap!" I shouted in a stage whisper-like tone, just missed the train. The gleaming digital sign hanging from the grimy ceiling above read 7 minutes until the next arrival. As any New Yorker would tell you, seven minutes in the Apple might as well be an eon.

The subway was empty. At best, there was a cockroach to keep me company. Leaning my head back in frustration against a tagged movie poster, I couldn't help but notice two shifty-looking guys pattering down the steps. To an outsider, this would seem weird, but this is Gotham. Weirdos are a dime a dozen. But it never hurts to be aware the shady duo slowly approached.

"Hey, cutie!" one shouted.

I could hear him through the low volume of my earbuds, my instincts influencing me to ignore him, but who isn't persistent in this city?

"Yo!" the other shouted in a more aggressive tone.

Best to just play along, so I removed one of my earbuds, only to give a ditsy response.

"Huh? Say something?" shouting as if my music were blaring.

"You got a cig I can bum?"

"Nah, sorry man, not much of a smoker," I candidly fired in my best hip non-ditsy white girl voice.

"What about a dollar?"

"Nah, don't carry cash," shrugging off his request.

At this point, it was probably best to detach myself from such a situation. I shifted down the platform, trying my best not to seem concerned about their attendance. Yet, just as my legs began to pivot, a tight grip clamped down on my wrist through my coat sleeve. I quickly snapped around to push the creep away, only to have his accomplice lock me in a bear hug from behind. Then, the punk in front of me proceeded to twist my arm. He was trying his best to remove my bag from my shoulder. Within the struggle, a kick was thrown at the loser, hitting him square in his nuts, and he doubled over in anguish. In my mind, kicking him should have granted me an opportunity to escape, but the others' grasp was far too strong. In a fit of rage, the ball-busted jerk rose from his fetal position, flipping open his jacket to

10

reveal a serrated blade the length of a screwdriver. At that moment, time seemed way too slow.

Spit was spewing from his mouth like a rabid hound barking, his upper and lower lips pressing together, simply to characterize me as a female dog. In the midst of my horror, I could see the dim subway lights waving and dancing across the shiny blade, only to hear the hum fluttering in the back of my ear canal. Sphhhlt! The hum went silent. The once shiny blade was now the color of ruby, each gulp of air now seeming like bent paper straw sips. Sphhhlt! Sphhhlt! Sphhhlt! My body fell into the void, eyes wide open, only to see stained white tiles before complete darkness.

Beep, beep, beep, beeeeep. "Hey! Move your car, you idiot. The light is green, idiot!"

"Hey, shut up! It's bumper to bumper, you moron!"

Beep, beep, beeeeep!

"STOP! Huff, huff, huff." I popped out of bed in a panic. That was a super odd dream, pressing my clammy hands to my face.

"Ugh," my hands fumbled around the items on my nightstand, shuffling for my phone with one eye closed tightly to a wink.

"God, what time is it?" I groaned before unlocking my phone.

"Oh, crap! 9 am! Crap, crap, crap! I am so late. Garrett is going to kill me."

Springing to my feet, still tightly wrapped in my floral comforter, I shed it like lizard skin, making a rush to the bathroom, but nothing could prepare me for what was about to happen next. Splashing the cool pedestal sink water to my face, my mind became fuzzy. The dream…the train station…those guys… was this real? Lowering my shaky hand, I gently touched my side only to detect a series of raised scars. Twinkling my fingers across the blemish like a grand pianist, a great migraine rumbled through my cerebral cortex.

"What the heck is wrong with me?" dropping to the floor in trauma.

My mind aimed for rational but extreme hunches. Was I…ya know … pregnant? No, that ain't it. You have to get action for that to happen; think smaller dummy. Maybe I drank a bit too much, but I don't recall going to a bar. As the pain persisted, I managed to pull myself to my feet, using my sink as if it were a walker.

"What happened? Where is this pain coming from? What the heck is going on?"

"Um, I think I can answer that," replied a mysterious voice.

Slowly lifting my head, my eyes went into a nystagmus state.

"Whhhhoo, who's there? You need to leave now, or I'm calling the cops!"

Tears and snot came trickling down my face. It was probably not a pretty sight.

"That's not going to do you any good," said the voice. *"Just give me a minute to explain, and promise not to freak out, okay?"*

Looking deeply into the tiny mirror just above the sink, the shape of a figure slowly walked towards me. At first, it was just a shadow, yet the closer it came, the more apparent it was.

"No, what the heck is going on? Someone drugged me! Al...Alvin!"

My hands clapped over my mouth in classic horror movie fashion, taking strides backward until tripping over the toilet, knocking over a clear plastic organizer. I sprang to my feet in fear and dashed out of the allegedly haunted apartment. Now, twisting and turning barefoot in my pajamas on a Midtown sidewalk, surely looking insane. Probably an understatement. This is New York, after all. As I scampered down the street, a voice zipped through my skull again.

"Phoebe! Please, Stop!" It shouted.

My sweaty palms quickly clapped over my buzzing ears. *"Stop it, stop it, stop it!"*

What the heck is going on? Suddenly, the towering buildings above went into a spin.

Thump...

"Lady, are you okay? Yo, Lady!" My eyes slowly opened, only to find a concierge looking down at me.

"Umm, I'm so sorry," I replied, flicking a coffee-stained napkin from my shoulder.

"Yeah, whatever, just get out of the trash! Aight, look. Usually, I'm supposed to report the crazies, but with pajamas like those, I'm just going to assume you're having a bad day." laughed the guard as he helped me out of the trash.

My PJs ... yeah, pretty snobbish looking.

"Yeah, you could say that, I guess. Thanks for the help...." I squinted my eyes as the once blurry text came into focus on his badge, *"Darius."*

"Anytime," he replied with a hint of coolness.

"Well, Darius, I'd better get going. It's freaking freezing out here ... And thanks again."

While walking up my apartment steps, my brain was trying its best to make sense of what had just happened. I slowly opened my door, peeking through the crack and scanning for a potential breach. Nothing, everything seemed quiet and clear, but better safe than sorry. Grabbing the ol' Slugger bat, I raised it as if I were at home plate. Skulking my way into the bathroom, the figure I once faced came into focus again in the mirror.

"Phoebe, it's me, Alvin. I know this is all too weird. I'm so sorry for creeping you out. But please let me explain."

I couldn't believe my eyes. It was definitely Alvin, mimicking and mirroring my every move.

"Oh my god, Alvin, it really is you!" *"Please tell me what's going on?"*

"Of course," said Alvin. *"But I highly suggest you take a seat."*

I took a gulp of the warm radiator air circulating the room, quickly exhaling, before plopping down on the toilet.

"Let me start with the most shocking part," sighed Alvin. *"Last night..."*

Oh no, whatever he was going to say was difficult. He took a deep huff as he slowly brushed his hand over his face.

"Last night..." Alvin sighed, raising my level of annoyance.

"Last night, what already?!" I shouted, tightly gripping the handle of my baseball bat in frustration.

"LAST NIGHT, YOU DIED! OKAY!" screamed Alvin from within the mirror, cringing in vexation.

My lips began to part, my jaw lowering in like a backhoe. Dead? I was completely unable even to spit out whole words.

"Di…di…died? I…I don't understand?" my gut began to bubble. I covered my mouth as my cheeks began to puff like a squirrel storing harvest.

Puke was coming up. At least I was near a sink. The disgust on Alvin's face said it all.

"Should I just stop here," winced Alvin.

"No, tell me everything! What exactly what's going on?" I asked, wiping my chin with my forearm.

"Okay, if you insist. Usually, I manage to get out of the office on time, but last night, it was as if everything that could delay me would. I knew I had missed the train by this time, so I stopped for a coffee. As I got closer to the station, I could hear the sounds of confrontation below the steps as the train rumbled away. As my foot touched down on the platform, I saw two guys going through the pockets of a lifeless body. There was blood everywhere."

As Alvin was speaking, my hand developed a mind of its own, touching the series of scars on my waist. My mind was twitching, thoughts from the previous night jumping in and out like a game of double Dutch.

Alvin continued, *"At this time, I was unaware that it was you. The thieves were rifling through a nearby bag. That's when I threatened to call the cops. They did not take my warning kindly. The duo began to rush towards my direction. Unfortunately for them, no bystanders were around, so I used magic to push them away. Guess that frightened them enough, as they bitterly retreated."*

Whoa, whoa, whoa… did this guy just say magic? I couldn't believe my ears! What on god's green earth was I hearing? Am I going insane?

"Alvin, this is all a bit much! This couldn't possibly be real! Am I going mental?"

Alvin looked at me with the most pitying expression.

"This is very real, and unfortunately, it's only going to get stranger. To my disbelief, the closer I got to the body, the more recognizable it became. You were cold, missing the spark from the day we met on the train. Your time was short. My first instinct was healing magic, but you were too far gone. In a last-ditch effort, I merged my essence into your body in order to restore your life. Now, here I am, a part of your very psyche."

I was at a loss for words. I sat on the toilet flat in expression, confused and oddly more alone than ever before. Then lightning struck, flaring the inquisitive part of my brain.

"So, Alvin, how did you get like this? The magic, the healing, the weird essence psyche thing? Who exactly are you?"

Alvin placed his hands into his pockets, slowly pacing from edge to edge of the now foggy mirror. It was obvious that this was a bit of a touchy subject for him, but I had to press the issue.

"Alvin!" I wailed, snapping him out of his brood.

"Right…answers! Sooo, my name is Alvin Casen.…I was born in 1798 to the oh-so-strict

parenting of Thomas and Allison Casen. My mother and father were both well-known real estate attorneys providing guidance to the most powerful landowners in New York. Naturally, my parents wanted one thing, and one thing only: for me to follow in their footsteps. Alas, I was different! I was into the arts, especially literature. By the time I was eighteen, I had already decided that law simply was not for me, thus pursuing a writing career. By twenty, I managed to land a job as a writer for a local tabloid paper. It was a small company, but, God, I loved it. I mean, sure, at the time, the paper was filled with fictitious tales and fabricated snake oil ads, but I had a true gift!"

As I sat listening to Alvin's story, I began to glow with child-like intrigue, like a little girl in a library listening to her favorite teacher read stories to a circle of young, spongy minds. I have to admit, for a girl who had died just last night, Alvin's tale was beginning to spark my own creative juices. His life seemed so poetic, a young man rebelling, Georgian era drama. This was the stuff that I wanted to read and edit!

Alvin continued his story. *"As time went on, I eventually ran into the hurdle that is writer's block."* He shrugged. *"My stories became dull. My tales were less captivating. My work began to suffer greatly. Shortly after, I was let go from my position at the tabloid. That's when I decided that I was going to write my own book, but first, I needed inspiration. Night after night, rummaging through countless studies and libraries. Researching epics, fantasies, and love stories written by the masters. But nothing pushed me, at least that, until I found 'it.' Locked away in a damp library cellar, the strange book resided. It was a tattered text, bound by leather buckles and straps, faded in pale green color. As I opened the book, I could tell by its contents that if I was found with this, it would mean the gallows for sure."*

"Gallows?"

"Well, yeah," said Alvin. *"It was the 1700s. Witchcraft was kinda like a big deal, but I digress ... I discovered that this text was more than just some weird book; it was a Night Script. It housed various spells and incantations, split into categories in various languages. Lucky for me, I was fluent in a few. At first, I started off with simple spells: a fire here, a light orb there. But I was thirsty for so much more. The deeper I dove into the Night Script, the more difficult it became to decipher. That didn't stop me, though. I soon discovered enchantment spells, possession spells, and even a spell to improve my focus and creativity. There was so much power at the tip of my fingers. At first, I thought I was just getting a touch ahead, but as time went on, I became a different person. Not knowing the dark secrets the Night Script truly held."*

This was intense, and I was on the edge of my now overly warm-toilet seat. What a story this was, but it explained a lot. I mean, the first time I met this guy, he had on shoes that cost more than my apartment and the furniture in it. He probably has wealth as old as his age, money coming out of the wazoo. Wait! If this guy is trapped in my mind, what happens to all of that moolah? Shallow thought, sure, but valid…right? I guess it couldn't hurt to ask. I did just die, after all.

"Soo…Alvin," I slowly coaxed. *"What is going to happen to your fortune now?"*

He began to slowly tap his upper lip in thought.

"Well, I had many safeguards put into place should I eventually meet my demise. So most of that will go to charity."

Charity, ugh, who wouldn't roll their eyes at his good-hearted nature?

"Figures, just my luck, I get possessed by a generous…a generous, come to think of it, what exactly are you? A ghost or something?"

Alvin lowered his head, taking a deep breath before speaking, seemingly annoyed by my rambling, and continued.

"As time went on, I started to realize that the more I used its magic, the more I was fading away. That's when I came across a spell that would grant me more life, 300 more years to be exact; definitely not what I was looking for. I just wanted something to counter my fading."

Fading away? What does that mean?

"As I deciphered the contents of the book further, I learned that it housed a great evil. Long ago, even before my time, two young maidens in a small upstate town known as Little Falls became infatuated with witchcraft. The legend goes that these two women grew tired of the oppressive nature of their significant others, but nonetheless, the word of man was law. One night, in order to exact their revenge, the two used witchcraft to summon a great Devil, only known as Gamigin."

"Hold it, friend, that's it for me!" I interrupted, jumping to my feet. Dying is one thing. Having my

body play host to some dude from the puffy shirt era is another. But Devils, absolutely not! No Devils, I was raised Catholic, ya know. Yet, the more I tried to convince myself, the more I became intrigued.

"So, what did this 'Gamigin' do?" I countered.

Alvin twisted his face into that of a grimace. *"Well... he did whatever the duo wished. He drove men to be infatuated with the sisters, slaying any villagers that would oppose them, mass amounts of wealth and power, you name it. However, power like that can't be controlled forever. Eventually, Gamigin rebelled and went rogue. You see, Devils crave one thing above all else, humans' dark desires, to build their strength and feed their Appetite. The human realm is plentiful. It didn't take long for the sisters to realize the just punishment served to those who had scorned them was feeding this devil beyond their control. The village and its occupants were on the brink of extinction. What good is power with no one to force your will upon? So, the decision was made to lock him away. "*

Gosh, I thought, fiddling my thumbs one over the other. That sounds intense. What the heck did I get myself mixed up with? At this point, a stiff drink was in order. I don't care if it was the a.m. or not. As I stood up to walk to the kitchen, I spotted Alvin's reflection in my hall mirror and then in the shine of the stainless-steel refrigerator. Christ, he was even reflecting through the dull polish of the silver toaster!

"Hey, what's the deal here? Are you just going to show up in anything with a reflection?" I questioned. *"Will I ever get to just see my own lovely face?"*

Alvin raised his hand, massaging the back of his neck in awkwardness, smiling at the comment.

"I'll get to that part, I promise, but I have a bit more to cover. Now, where was I? Oh yes, I remember. So, with Gamigin out of control, the sisters decided to send him back to his realm. But he was far too strong. At least, that was until his weakness was discovered. See, unlike the movies, Devils aren't allergic to light or holy water. That's all made up, as you truly can't kill a Devil. So you do the next best thing: trap them or convince them to return home by revealing their true name."

I quickly chugged my glass of morning liquor, wincing from the burn of amber-colored Scotch. I was in a state of shock, still convincing myself that all of this nonsense was just a dream. I reached for my phone, and five missed calls were all from Garrett. He's probably worried sick that I'm not in the office yet. I decided to give Garrett a ring, putting on an Oscar-worthy "I'm so sick" performance. My day was shot, and work was definitely out of the cards.

"So, how did they do it?" I stressfully asked Alvin, wiping the droplets of liquor from my chin.

"Well, according to legend, the sisters trapped him within the confines of this book, which is only a means of keeping a Devil at bay. But pages are missing, and it's never made clear if the sisters discovered his true name or which spell was used."

I quickly let out a gasp of relief. At first, I thought this was going to end with the classic, *"and now he's loose upon the world trope."* Alas, nope, it looks like no danger in sight. Other than Ghost Boy here stuck in my psyche, I'd say I'm in the clear.

"Okay, so you're saying that this Gamigin is still trapped in that weird book, right? So, no real danger?" I asked.

Alvin's face had a look of reservation. *"Well..."*

"Well, what?" I roared as I poured my second glass of liquor.

"Remember how I mentioned the Night Script's dark secrets and the feeling of fading away? Well, it turns out the magic being used requires human desires, which give power to Gamigin. The greater the magic, the larger the desire, the greater the feed. If he consumes enough energy, he could free himself of the book."

I could tell by Alvin's face that he felt a sense of guilt. All of those years of using magic, powering a Monster unknowingly, heck, I couldn't imagine. Yet, I couldn't help but wonder one thing.

"Alvin, why did you risk yourself to save me?" I asked, gazing into the reflective toaster.

"I guess I did it because it was the right thing to do. When the healing magic didn't work, I panicked. It was time for plan B.

Alvin pointed his finger in my direction in the shape of a gun. *"Melding magic, everybody wins. You stay alive, and my consciousness doesn't become Devil food."*

"Melding Magic," I murmured, *"how does that work?"*

"Well, it's actually pretty simple," Alvin replied. *"Melding Magic takes one life-force and merges it with another. That's it! At least, in theory, the complexity of the spell itself is another story."*

Complexity, huh? I could only wonder how this spell was really going to affect me in the long run.

"So, question Alvin, does this mean that I can use magic?" I said with a mischievous grin, curving from cheek to cheek like the Christmas Grinch. Alvin shook his head in yes fashion, but his face spelled rebuke.

"Have you not heard anything I've said?" lobbed Alvin with the disapproval of a stern parent.

"Are you trying to set Gamigin free? Absolutely no magic! It's far too risky, and besides, magic takes years to master. Just be glad you're alive and end it there."

I felt like a child being scolded by a teacher. I couldn't believe it! Here I am with unlimited access to Harry Potter Level sorcery that could literally change my life, and I'm not allowed to use it. As I peered into the reflection, I could see Alvin's lips moving, but honestly, his warning was raining down on deaf ears. He might as well have been the teacher in Charlie Brown, "wah-wah-wah-wah." I mean, it took centuries to drain Alvin's life force. Surely, just a few spells wouldn't be enough to power this Gamigin character, right? Alvin's words came back into focus. I shook my head and began to nod in approval. I zoned out. All I kept thinking about were the possibilities.

Alvin's voice came crashing back into my skull like a brick with a note tied to it, smashing through my cerebrum window.

"Phoebe, Phoebe, promise me, you won't use magic under any circumstance, okay?"

I stood up, turning my back on the metallic toaster, only to see Alvin's reflection scanning me from the kitchen window reflection. Well, I guess he's the expert here, fine.

"I promise, Alvin. No magic."

Chapter Two

The Viceroy

osh! How could today possibly top yesterday? Here I am, back on the disgusting train, heading back to the office, only to bow and smile to my annoying overlords. Not to mention fixing the endless pages of dribble scattered across my desk for Trembly's new piece of Hollywood trash. If they only knew what I had been through! I mean, I literally just died!

"Wow, someone is in a salty mood," shot Alvin's voice through my skull.

"Jesus Christ, Alvin, I nearly wet myself! Can you please let me know when you're going to just pop up?" I shouted aloud.

A cluster of people began to stare and whisper. I lowered my head, my cheeks cardinal from embarrassment.

"Well, this is my stop," I whispered, followed by a series of awkward laughs. I clutched my bag and dashed up the station steps.

"Hey AL-VIN!" I shakingly snapped.

"Well, 'ello madame," joked Alvin in a horrible British accent.

"Okay, one, never do that voice again," I laughed, watching the cold condensation flow out of my mouth, *"and two, would it kill you to…I don't know…*

let me know when you're going to jump into my brain. I mean, half of New York now thinks I'm a flossy, crazy person," I sarcastically stated as I walked expeditiously to Monarch.

"And while we were on the topic of our little union, must you pop up in every reflective surface in my vicinity? Do you have any idea how hard it is to do my makeup with your reflection constantly in the way?"

I could hear Alvin's laugh permeating through my mind, bouncing side to side like that pixelated ball in Pong.

"Wait, you're wearing makeup, hmmm?" joked Alvin.

I couldn't help but laugh at his kittenish humor. I felt like that girl in high school who had found that one male friend that they were the most comfortable around. It was almost, dare I say it, crush-like.

"So what are you trying to say, Alvin? I don't know how to wear makeup, or I'm not wearing enough. In my defense, I've never really been more than an eyeliner girl."

Alvin began to chuckle. *"Or maybe you're so pretty that I didn't even notice the makeup,"* said Alvin in a smooth radio talk voice.

"Oh, that's a good one," I winked, *"but again, your imitations and accents need work."* I snickered.

"Ouch," spat Alvin, *"that hurts! But seriously, Phoebe, if you do ever need... ya know, psyche alone time, just say the magic words, and away I go."*

"The magic words? I thought I wasn't allowed to use magic," rolling my eyes to the heavens as I knew I was about to endure a long-drawn-out explanation.

"Correct," said Alvin, *"no magic. But should you ever need alone time, simply spout the word 'Tu et ego,' and you're back in the driver's seat."*

Oddly enough, I had heard this language before. It was Latin, if I'm not mistaken. One of the first projects I ever worked on at Monarch was a history book that was focused on the Roman Republic. I'm no etymology professor, but I knew a thing or two.

"Tu et ego…hum, seems easy enough. Anything to escape your bad imitations, right Alvin…Alvin?

What the heck is going on? Literally, two seconds ago, I couldn't shut up *Sam Wheat* here. Now, he's gone! My mind grew hazy again like the morning after my death, jumping back and forth, struggling to focus. It was like an out-of-body experience, my very being slipping into disarray. It truly felt like a piece of me had gone missing.

"Alvin…you can come back now!" I shouted like a panicked parent searching for their child after a game of hide and seek gone wrong.

"Seriously, Alvin, I get it. Come back, please come back!" Oh, God! Did I offend him? I swear I didn't mean the things I said!

"This is so stupid!" I screamed, dropping to a cold nearby bench. *"I should have never said it! Stupid Tu et ego!"*

Like licking a battery, I felt a sudden jolt in my cortex.

"Wow, that was weird," said Alvin's voice, slowly dissolving back into my consciousness.

"Oh my god, Alvin, you're back!" I shouted, completely unfazed by onlookers' confusion. *"Where did you go? I was…."*

"Worried?" said Alvin in a haughty tone. *"Just think of it as a way of putting me to sleep on command. Kinda like a virtual assistant or something."*

"Sleep! Are you serious right now?" I stood up from the bench, crossing my arms like a spoiled child, only to quickly realize that I had to dial it back a bit. I was letting too many emotions show. I'm not one to act so smitten.

"Yes, sleep," Alvin replied. *"You see when I used Melding Magic to revive you, we became one. However, once the spell is cast, the spellcaster must adhere to the rules of the incantation. That rule is quite simple: the physical host is in charge, my friend. So, technically, you're not using magic. You're just enforcing rules. But be careful with this, remember we are one. You can't exist without me, and I can't exist without you. If I'm put to sleep for too long, your body will begin to shut down. The body and mind must be one."*

Must be one? What is this Jedi crap! Nevertheless, enforcing the rules huh? Well, I must say that is certainly a relief. I looked at the digital numbers on my watch. I guess we better get moving. I can't afford to fall behind any further with Trembly's great manifesto. Yuck, I thought, slowly ruffling my nose as if I could smell my own B.S. in the air. Before I knew it, I was at the Monarch's front door.

"Okay, Alvin, I'm afraid this is where we part ways. I've got a lot of work to catch up on, and I need as little distraction as possible."

God, I felt like my father, minus the crescendo.

"Hey, say less, my friend," replied Alvin, with the coolness of the Fonz. *"But hey, Pheebs, before I forget, I need a tiny, tiny favor."*

Oh great, a favor. Now, not only is this guy living rent-free in my mind, but he's gonna start mooching, too. Yet, I couldn't be too upset. He did save my life, after all.

"Okay…let's hear it, what is this so-called favor?"

"Perfect!" declared Alvin. *"So, after work, I need you to go to my apartment and gather a few important items of mine before they are collected for charity."*

That's right, this all makes sense. I totally forgot this guy is loaded, and now, well…he's gone, like smoke in the wind. Then it hit me! A lot of questions are going to be asked. I mean, he's literally a missing person.

"So Alvin, I assume the authorities are going to be looking for you. How the heck is this all going to be explained?"

Somehow, I could discern Alvin's movements in my brain, smirking his face with a slight twang of arrogance.

"Not to worry," said Alvin. *"It's all taken care of. My caretaker has specific instructions in the event of my disappearance. He knows exactly what to say and do. As far as everyone will know, I sold my apartment, donated everything in it, and moved abroad. Piece of cake. I'm wealthy, not famous. Well, I was wealthy, at least."*

I hate to admit it, but he's right. Wealthy people pick up and leave all the time. What's one more to the mix? I sighed in concession.

"Well... what am I grabbing, and how exactly do I get in?"

"Getting in is going to be a bit tricky. No way the doorman is just going to let you waltz in. It's not like he can call me to confirm," said Alvin in a whisper.

"Why the heck are you whispering, you idiot? No one but me can hear you. Just talk."

I mumbled out the side of my mouth like a ventriloquist. Giving the fakest of smiles to people in passing.

"I got it!" shouted Alvin. *"The doorman knows that I love my Thai food. Just pick up an order of my usual, then when you get to the front desk, he'll send you right up."*

"Great Plan, Genius, but when I get to your apartment, how do I get in?" I fired back.

"What? Are you serious?" replied Alvin with a suck of his teeth. *"I'll give you the key code, duh!"*

Oh yeah, that is right. I keep forgetting that this guy is rich, unlike the other commoners with our lowly keys.

"Okay, then what am I grabbing?" I whispered.

Alvin seemed to go radio silent, his thoughts percolating like bubbles popping out of brewing coffee. Then, he spoke.

"We'll cross that road when we get there," said Alvin in a more serious tone.

"Oh, come on, you can't just leave me hanging." I joked with an oh-so-subtle hint of seriousness.

"Well, worry about that later!" snapped Alvin, this time adding a bit of base to his tone. Gone was the flirtatious humor from before and replaced with the Russian Roulette-like seriousness.

"I'm sorry. I didn't mean to be so rude. Umm, how about we pick up here later on after work? I know you've got a lot to accomplish today with that Timber guy," said Alvin with a laugh.

"Sure thing…Later on then… I better get inside, Al. This is where we part."

A bit of sadness came over me at that moment. I knew something was bothering him, but what could it be? God, I was doing it again, having another stupid crush moment! I always had a thing for the mysterious type, but now's not the time. The tears were coming, and I didn't really want to go to Monarch today. I wanted to stay with him. Yet, with the faintness of a mouse's whisper, I rolled the hex from my dry mouth to my glossy lips, each word swerving through the Big Apple-abiding racket.

"Tu et ego."

Just like that, Alvin was gone. I paused for a minor moment, clutching my computer bag before storming into the lobby. Everything was silent in my head for once. With each step, I could hear the sound of my clogged boots scraping Monarch's mirror-finished floor. When I arrived at the elevator, I only saw my reflection; there was no Alvin in sight. I need to get a grip! He's practically not even a real person, but even so, I knew what was happening. I was falling for him, as crazy as that sounds. Just as I went to press the up button, the silver elevator doors zipped open. It was Garrett leaning in the corner pocket of the elevator with the swagger of Harry Palmer.

"Kiddo, welcome back, how ya feeling?" exhaled Garrett.

Like a 12th grader who watched her crush get asked to homecoming by another girl. *"Great,"* I replied with a fake Cheshire cat smile! *"Just a little bug, but I'm good!"*

"Glad to hear it," said Garrett with his classic thumbs up. *"Let's knock this Trembly piece out of the park. Remember, you and I have big bets riding on this one."*

That's right! Here, I am being selfish, and I totally forgot what Garrett has at stake. Not to mention, he has so much faith in my talents and abilities that he's willing to take me to the next level with him. When the elevator whizzed open, I could already hear the endless office banter. God, do I really have to do this today? And to make matters worse, all I could hear were my own thoughts, ugh!!

"Phoebe, Phoebe!" Garrett's voice came swirling through my ear like that of a fuzzy Q-Tip.

"You still there, kiddo?" said Garrett with a chuckle.

"Get yourself a hot cup of Joe, and let's knock this sucker out. Also, before I forget, we have a new intern today. I want you to show her the ropes a bit."

Like a flaming meteorite, the word *intern* crash landed on my brain's frontal lobe. Perking my ears up like that collie dog on that old TV show.

"Wait...what? No, Garrett. Not an intern. Don't I have enough work as is?" I whined.

"Sorry, kiddo, Chris calls the shots, and he wants someone to fill that assistant editor position ASAP. So, why not pinch the penny with an intern," said Garrett.

"But I have no idea what the previous assistant was working on. How in the world did this fall in my lap?" I scowled, pleading my case as we walked in stride.

"Just show her around and find an assignment for her," shrugged Garrett. *"Coffee, staff, supply room. I already met her; she's very easygoing, and it's only for this week, so then she's out of your hair. Her name is Louise. She's waiting for you in your office."*

I released a loud, immature huff, scruffing my way past glass office after office. But the truth is, it wasn't the intern that was bothering me… It wasn't even Trembly's stupid book… It was going through Alvin withdrawal, plain and simple. Sulking through the halls, I could see the new intern sitting quietly in my office, gently brushing her bouncy spring of a curl out of the scope of her vision. She had big, beautiful brown eyes, with skin the color of honey. It reminded me of that upside-down bear in my kitchen cabinet. She wore thick black glasses, sporting a sleeveless houndstooth dress. One of her arms was covered in tattoos from her wrist to the top of the humerus, with curly gingerbread hair resting in a bun upon the top of her head. Wow, I must be really hungry, describing a human with food, but even I could see that she was very attractive. Leave it to Chris to hire with his eyes and not his brain. Oh well! Time to crank up the facade as she slowly began to rise to her feet.

"Why, hello! You must be Louise. My name is Phoebe, and…welcome to Monarch Publishing!" Holy crap, there was my inner white girl flaring up again. Just be normal.

"It is so nice to meet you," Louise replied. *"Garrett has told me so much about you!"* placing her free hand earnestly across her heart.

"Hopefully, all good things," I replied with an awkward giggle. An uncomfortable pause fell between us. Okay, maybe I felt a smidge intimidated. I mean, she's young, pretty, and eager. It's not like she was gunning for my job or anything, but I guess this is how the only child feels when a new sibling comes along.

"Well, how's about I give you the grand tour!"

After about 45 minutes, I was back in my office. I managed to scrounge up things to keep Louise busy for the remainder of the day. And finally, I had a chance to lean into this stupid book. What a train wreck this all was. I was getting nowhere… seconds turned to minutes, and minutes turned to hours. I was running out of coffee and fingernails to bite, and still, no luck working my magic on this crap. I knew today's work was going to make a guest appearance in my apartment tonight. I looked up at the clock that had been mocking me all day. It was finally time to roll out. But this evening felt different because as soon as that elevator hit floor one. I spit those magic words out like stale chewing gum.

"Tu et ego!"

I could hear a great, big yawn echoing through my head.

"Well, that was definitely the nap I needed," said Alvin's voice in a groggy tone. *"How was the office today, Pheebs?"*

I couldn't believe how excited I was to hear his stupid voice. I could barely force out complete sentences.

"Umm… work, yeah it was…it was…"

Clearly, the cat had my tongue. Heck, more like a Tiger, I felt like a complete moron.

"Was it good? Bad? Productive?" Questioned Alvin. *"Oh, I get it, ya missed me, huh?"*

And just like that, I snapped out of my trance. *"Me…ahha…miss you? I think not, my friend. If anything, I'm just excited about our little mission this evening."* All things considered, I think I played off my excitement pretty well. *"So what's the plan, Stan?"*

"Right, the plan!" said Alvin. *"So, first things first, we need to catch the D train to my apartment. Quick, take this address down on your phone. 100 1/2 W 31st St."*

Panic and urgency were the tone of Alvin's voice.

"Ooh la la, aren't we fancy? Mister, I live a stone's throw away from Herald Sq," I joked. Alvin was so excited that the sarcasm flew right past him.

"Once you get to my side of town, go to the corner and look for a Thai shop called The Lucky Banana Leaf. Just say that you're picking up for Alvin. They know my order like the backs of their hands."

In no time at all, I found myself heading down the steps to catch the train. Something was wrong. With each step, I could feel a sense of dread making its way deeper and deeper into my gullet.

This was the first time since my initial death that I had been in the subway station at this hour. I couldn't help but to think the worst. The bottom of the steps seemed as if it had gone on forever. All I could imagine is being murdered...again. I covered my ears while dropping to a crouching position. If I tucked my knees to my stomach any further, I might turn into an armadillo. I was having a bit of a panic attack.

"I...I...I don't think I can go down there," I whispered.

"Hey, hey, hey! Take a deep breath. Breathe, you can do this, Phoebe," said Alvin in a tranquil tone. *"I got your back. I won't let anything happen to you."*

There was a bit of reassurance, knowing that Alvin was with me this time. I picked myself up and began to make my descent. One foot after another, at the pace of a toddler, I eventually made my way underground. As I stood on the platform, I noticed how jittery it made me at this hour. Every gust of wind from passing trains, the rattling of soda cans in a homeless person's bag, and even the sight of the yellow edge line made me jumpy. I placed my back against a digital advertisement, only to notice a man walking towards me at a hasty pace. Not only was he getting closer, but his hand was in his jacket pocket.

My body was locking up, and I was breathing so hard I could hear whistling coming from my nostrils. Was he going to kill me too? Out of the blue, he stopped dead in his tracks and removed his hand from his jacket, only to reveal a phone. He was glancing simultaneously between it and the subway map. I rubbed my hands over my exhausted eyes, titled my head back, and let out a great exhale.

"Easy Pheebs, everything is fine. You're doing great, and look, the train is even here on time."

36

I quickly jumped aboard the packed car, scanning for a place to sit. As we approached our stop, all of my anxiety and stress dissolved like a pinch of sugar in a glass of hot Oolong. I heard once that it's the anticipation of the journey that makes the trip long. That statement couldn't have been more accurate than right now. As I reached the peak of the raunchy subway steps, I couldn't have been more relieved. I sipped the crisp air, thinking it was back to the mission at hand. I pulled out my mobile and began to place an order.

"Hello. Lucky Banana Leaf. Pick up or delivery?" Asked the receptionist.

Based on my nervousness, one would have thought that I had never placed an order before.

"Umm...Hey...yeah, so I would...Umm, like to, palace and order for pick up...I guess?"

"Sure..." said the receptionist, with an uncertain tone. *"What will it be?"* I'm sure she could smell my ditziness through the phone.

I could hear Alvin whispering his usual order inside of my head. This is a lot of food. Who orders this much food for one is all I could think of. Alvin could tell my nerves were in full control as I messed up the order several times, confusing the daylights out of the poor woman on the other end of the line. Alvin's patience was wearing thin. *"Just say it's an order for Alvin Casen,"* he puffed.

Right... *"Actually, this is an order for Alvin Casen."* I quickly spat. I began biting my lower lip and squinting my eyes, with hopes of his name being some sort of magic word. The line abruptly went silent, and only I could mess up something as simple as an order.

"...Oh, okay!" shouted the receptionist. *"You should have just said so. It should be ready in about 15 minutes. Please tell Mr. Casen to enjoy a complimentary bottle of wine. It's on the house."*

I hung up the phone, only to be more confused than when I started.

"Complimentary wine?" Who exactly was this guy? That is a fair question, as I never truly took the time to do my own research on him.

"Okay," started Alvin. "The *Lucky Banana Leaf* should be right on Fifth Ave. Let's roll out!"

As we strolled the blocks, making our way to the restaurant, I couldn't help but let my mind get the best of me. Who exactly was Alvin? Was everything he told me legit? It never really dawned on me. In my defense, I was dead just two days ago, and I was still shaking off the shock of the situation. I know he told me that he was born in the 1700s to a pair of strict parents. Nevertheless, I was blindly following a stranger into God knows what. My pace began to slow, unable to focus on finding the restaurant and walking at the same time.

"Hey, Pheebs, there it is. Just pop in and grab the food, and then it's off to my place."

Off to my place? I think I see what is going on here. Food for at least two people. If I had to guess, this was his usual Playboy special. The nerve of this guy!

"So, do all the ladies get this treatment?" I mumbled as I picked up the order of prepaid food. And here I am, thinking I was just a little special.

"What's that supposed to mean?" replied Alvin with stupefaction in his tone.

"Just…Never mind, let's just get going." Obviously, I was a bit jealous, and I wasn't doing the best job of hiding it at the moment. I was battling a whirlwind of confusing thoughts in my head. Alvin, who was he really? Was I just another girl who he was unfortunately stuck with this time? What am I saying? He's not some guy. He's more like a symbiote or something like Venom, only a heck of a lot nicer.

We finally reached our destination. A grand, towering building, hiding its utmost levels well within the nighttime fog. Walking into the lobby, I couldn't help but feel like a peasant. The bone-white colored floor shined and glistened under the sparkly chandelier swaying above. A great piano sat in the middle of the lobby, playing away with a mind of its own. As I looked to the other side of the lobby, I spotted an antique grandfather clock nestled perfectly between a smooth green suede divan and a wingback chair.

"Oh no!" shouted Alvin.

"What's wrong?" I whispered as I slowly approached the front desk.

"This isn't good." He replied. *"The doorman, I don't recognize him! Crap, Jorge must have switched his hours. This new guy will never let you upstairs without my approval."*

Great, this so-called plain was going south really fast. As I drew closer to the front desk, the doorman slowly raised his head, revealing his face from the shadow of his Chauffeur hat.

"Wait! Alvin, I know that guy!"

"You know him?" said Alvin. *"Know him from where?"*

"From the day after my death!" I gasped. *"When I spiraled out, once I came back to my senses, he was the guard that helped me out of a heap of trash. I'm pretty sure his name is…"*

"Darius!" I blurted out, quickly slapping my hands over my mouth in embarrassment.

He glanced in my direction, tilting his head to the side in confusion.

"Do I know you?" replied Darius, shifting a package to the corner of the grand lobby desk.

"Oh wait, I remember you. You're 'Pajamas,' right?" Joked Darius, brandishing the handsomeness of Colgate smiles.

"Ha Ha, very funny. Glad I left such a good impression. So… what are you doing here? I thought you worked in Midtown."

Darius shrugged his shoulders with the coolness of a high school team captain.

"Well, ya know, same company, different building, a little extra bread in my pocket. I guess I could ask you the same thing. You, ah DoorDash?"

"DoorDash?" I replied, only to remember the order of hot Thai food in my hand, its glorious smell wafting from the clear plastic bag.

"Oh this, um no, this is…actually for a…friend that lives in this um building." I could feel myself blushing. I'm not sure what it was, but I felt like I was talking to a famous person or something. I couldn't stop smiling.

"A friend, huh?" joked Darius. *"Well, what is this 'friends' name? I'll let him or her know you're here."*

Alvin, who had been strangely quiet for the most part, quickly chimed in.

"No! Just tell him it's a surprise. Don't want to ruin it."

"Um, actually, can I just take the food up to him? It's a bit of a surprise."

Darius sucked his teeth, followed by a cheeky grin. Oh no, here it goes: do or die.

"Well. Technically, we're supposed to notify all tenants. But… aight, just these one-time PJs. Can't be risking my job, ya know. And, save me some," smiled Darius. *"Take elevator number two."*

I bowed as if he was some sort of royal, thanking him as I backpedaled into the elevator.

"Wow! You two seem chummy," said Alvin in a snippy tone.

"Don't be jealous," I fired. *"We made it in, didn't we? Now, which floor are we going to?"*

"Yeah, whatever you say," replied Alvin, with all sorts of sour oozing out of his voice.

"Anywho, we're going all the way up! Lucky number 23."

As we reached the top floor, the clean steel doors crept open. If I didn't know any better, I would have thought I had died…well again, and went to heaven. I had to rub my eyes in amazement. This wasn't just an apartment. This was a bachelor pad on steroids…It was truly the apogee of wealth. Even so, amongst all of the razzle-dazzle and fat-cat affluence, I had even more questions about Alvin now than I'd ever had before.

Chapter Three
Swallowtail

I would like to think that I knew what struggle was. I mean, my family wasn't rich, but on the flip side of this coin, we weren't poor. I had just enough with my own fair share of ups and downs. They are not the newest sneakers, but they are not off-brand, not Alexander McQueen boots, but definitely Doc Martens, no Jordan's, but definitely Air Force Ones. As I looked around Alvin's lair, I slowly began to realize the vast gap between the middle class and wealth. I mean, this guy had it all! Drifting from the elevator into the living area, I couldn't help but notice the 75-inch T.V. Alvin mocking me within the screen's reflection, sticking out his tongue with the charm of a seven-year-old. Panning from left to right, Alvin's odd taste in decor jumped out from all directions. Think industrial modern meets geek, the perfect blend.

The furniture was sleek and sterile, yet the decorations were old and odd. Everything was perfectly combined, from a rotary phone dial on the reflective futuristic-looking metal table to the movie-size posters dimly lit on the hallway walls with motion sense lighting resembling Edison bulbs. I respected it; it was clean, neat, and a far cry from the chaos in my apartment. But the time for admiration has passed. I was here on a mission.

"Okay, where am I going, Al? What am I looking for?" I spouted as I scuffed through the palatial apartment.

"Right," said Alvin in a woeful tone. *"Sorry, Phoebe, I got a bit nostalgic for a moment. Just finally hit me that all of my treasures are going to go away,"* said Alvin as I picked up a vintage Optimus Prime figure from his large oak desk.

"Well, if it helps, I'd be more than willing to take some of these collectibles off your hands." I joked with a pepper of seriousness.

"It can't hurt, I suppose. If you see anything you like, feel free." Groaned Alvin. *"It's probably better in your hands anyway. But before you ransack my apartment,"* he snickered, *"let's get what we came here for."*

Alvin began to guide me through the twists and turns of the monstrous flat. Down a long hallway, past an interminable table with seating for 12 or more and bookcases stretched to the heavens. Each shelf was congested with literature from various time periods. Eventually, we reached what seemed to be a fancy globe of sorts nestled in the corner. This was far from your average high school classroom globe. It was hand-painted, its wooden base polished to a reflective shine with a dark lacquer. Combine that with the feet of some sort of lion, and you have a pricey regal piece.

"Okay, Phoebe. I need you to spin the globe in the exact sequence I tell you."

Oh! This is fun, kinda like Scooby Doo or something. What's next, the creeper behind a gold sconce?

"Left, right, right, down, up, down, counterclockwise spin," said Alvin, seemingly unsure of the correct sequence.

Without delay, the equator of the globe split, releasing a sizzle followed by a puff of stale dust. I noticed a tiny silver hinge that sat above Africa, in which I flicked it with the precision of a smoker tossing a bud. As I reached my hand through the dwindling cloud of white smoke, there it was: a dusty, rigid white box. Just as I began to reach for the lid, Alvin quickly interjected.

"Phoebe, wait!"

My hand halted as if Alvin himself grabbed my wrist.

"Before you open the box, just remember what you promised me: No magic! What's in this box is extremely dangerous. It's not another toy and must be protected and feared at all cost."

"Of course." I nodded, but who the heck was I kidding? I was as excited as a puppy finding a new home.

I could feel my palms becoming gooey with sweat as I slowly peeled the lid back. What was in this box? Gold, a secret diary, a family heirloom like a locket or ring hiding some sort of key? As you can see, my childish mind was running wild. Boy, was I wrong! Inside the box was a small greenish book, held together by tattered brown leather straps and rusty old buckles. I couldn't believe what I was looking at! It's the book from Alvin's story…that *Night Script* thing.

Let's just say this: I had never been more excited and disappointed at the same time. I could feel my stupid face forming, a face usually reserved for pics I receive from guys that I have met on dating apps.

"Well, Phoebe, there it is," said Alvin, followed by a gulp in his throat. *"The Night Script."*

"This little thing!" I immediately hurled, *"This is the Night Script? What a rip-off, you can't be serious!"*

"What the heck are you talking about?" Countered Alvin. *"This is the most powerful and dangerous book on the face of the Earth, and you're worried about its appearance?"*

"I mean, yeah, sure, I get that, Al. But I was just expecting something... Ya know."

"No, I don't know Phoebe! Please enlighten me on your masterful knowledge of spell books!"

"Hey, don't get moody. I was just simply saying that I was expecting something a little bit more, I don't know... bigger. Like the stuff you see in the movies, this thing is the size of a 90s Talkback Dear Diary."

"Well, I'm sorry, spellbooks don't meet your awe-inspiring motif," snarled Alvin.

"Look, I'm sorry, Phoebe, I didn't mean to be so snappy. It's just that this is a very dangerous book, and it's my duty to make sure it never falls into the wrong hands, which brings me to my next bullet point. Phoebe, I need you to promise me two things. Please never utter a word of this text. I know I sound like a broken record, but you must believe me."

I nodded my head in agreement. He had a bit of a point. I'm no spellbook expert, and I was a bit out of my league here.

"Second, once we get back to your place, I need you to hide this box. As far as I'm concerned, it should never see the light of day."

"Why not just burn it, Al?" A quick thought that seemed logical, even as I lobbed it out of my mouth.

Alvin began to chuckle a smidge, an emotion much more welcomed than his uptight paranoia.

"I wish it was that easy, Phoebe. Believe me, I've tried." He laughed. *"But magic this evil and powerful can't be so easily snuffed out. I think we have everything. We should probably get going."*

As I lifted the box out of the globe, a stale piece of paper with a sketch of a beautiful young woman lay underneath it. I picked up the photo with my free hand, blowing off the dust to admire its artistic craftsmanship.

"Wow, this is amazing!" The inking and the attention to detail are all exquisitely jaw-dropping. I felt like I was looking at something Jack drew for Rose.

"Who is she, Alvin?" I questioned, trying my best to keep an inquisitive tone, all while trying not to seem too impressed like a snobbish art curator.

It was odd. I could feel a warming sensation within my mind. Alvin's emotions seemingly began to flow through my body as if they were my own. He was happy, but that sensibility quickly shifted to sadness.

"No one of importance," purred Alvin.

Odd if she's not important, then why keep a drawing of her?

"Wow, she's gorgeous!"

"Yeah, her employees would say only on the outside," joked Alvin.

"*Allison The Devil was the nickname given to her. But enough about her. Let's take what we have and get going."*

Packing up the rigid box, I made my way back to the elevator. As the floors began to sink in digits, I quickly realized that I couldn't just waltz out of this building holding a box. Time to run an audible. I discarded the package in a nearby trash bin, shoving the *Night Script* in my laptop bag along with the picture. As the elevator door clanked open, Darius was at the front desk shooting the breeze with another tenant.

"Enjoy your day, Mr. Clark. Hey, Hey, Hey, where are you going, leaving so soon?" I tried to dart past him, but seriously, the charm of this guy was magnetic.

"I guess that spicy Thai food is affecting your hearing?"

I turned around, trying my damndest not to crack a smile from lobe to lobe. Darius had a similar effect to Alvin, but he was real, live, and in person, not just a voice in my head.

"If you must know, friend, I don't eat Thai food." That's a lie p.s.

"I'm more of a taco truck kinda girl."

"Tacos…." said Darius with an inquisitor's 'ahh.'

"Well, good thing I like taco trucks, too. And it just so happens that tomorrow is my off day. Care to join?"

"Are you asking me out?"

47

Oh my God. I sound so stupid. That's exactly what he's doing. I just have to keep my focus. Focus on his eyes, his big brown enchanting eyes.

"I guess so. I mean, who could turn down a good taco?" Darius shrugged.

I tapped my index against my chin as if I hadn't made up my mind 15 seconds ago.

"I'll think about it. How about you give me your cell and I'll keep you in the loop."

I must admit. I was very proud of myself for keeping such good composure.

"Fair enough," smiled Darius, with his beautiful white teeth. I placed his number on my mobile, trying my hardest not to mess up. My hand grazed his hand as I went to give him his phone back. I will never wash this hand again and, of course, leave it to some wealthy jerk to spoil the moment.

"Darius, oh, Darius!" cried a snobbish voice from within the elevator.

"Guess that's my cue. Hope to hear from you Pajamas," said Darius as he jogged away to assist.

"Umm hello, are we done here?" Whoops, I forgot I had affairs to attend to with Alvin. *"Now that you're all done drooling over lover boy. Can we get back home and finish up, please?"*

Wow, someone is being pushy. But in Alvin's defense, I guess I would be a little jealous if he did the same, at least in normal life. But my life has been far from normal for the past few days, and I don't see that changing anytime soon. As I made my way to the top of the stairs, one clear matter of fact hit me: I'm probably the worst person trusted to hide this stupid book. I suck at hiding things! My mother would always find anything I stashed away, and now I'm tasked with hiding a dangerous spell book. Great. I began to scour my little cove, looking for any innocuous place to hide the hellish transcript, choosing all of the basics, only to have them shot down by Alvin's criticism.

"Closet? Top shelf!" I acclaimed.

"No way!" hurled Alvin, *"Way too easy, way too obvious."*

"Wait, I got it! How about under the sink?"

"Ehh...Still seems a bit insecure," he groaned.

This back-and-forth went on for hours. They say you can learn a lot about a person by living with them. Well, try having that person live inside your mind. Alvin is picky. Combine that with adamantine, and you have one tough cookie. I've never met Alvin's mother, but based on the past few hours, this apple didn't fall far from the tree. I was spent, out of ideas, zapped, I tell you. I was convinced that in this apartment, there had been no stone left unturned and still no hiding spot, or at least that was until I plopped down on my rickety old couch.

"This is just imposs.... Wait...wait, wait, wait!"

I twisted my head to the side like a confused pet. *"There it is..."* right in front of me, so obvious yet so inconspicuous. A small little slit between the stove and the counter, just wide enough for my hand to pierce and place the *Night Script*. I think it's perfect, but what does Lord Hide and Seek think?

"Alvin, I got it between the stove and the counter. Nothing is going in there but crumbs and roaches." I had that percolating feeling in my skull again. Alvin was thinking.

49

"Hum, that's not bad. It seems like it goes pretty far back. And from the looks of it, you'd need relatively small hands to access it. I think we've got our spot."

In the midst of containing my shock, I removed the tiny book along with Allison's portrait from the zipper pocket of my laptop. Placing it gently on the counter, I proceed to wrap the book and fragile drawing like a priest preparing a body for mummification. Shining my cell phone light between the gap, I couldn't help but notice every little toast and Poptart crumb of yesteryear, that and an abandoned butter knife, gross! No wonder the roaches love it here, but this is definitely it. You would have to be pretty desperate to get on your hands and knees to find this puppy hidden here. As I watched the book slide back into the skinny void, a side of me couldn't seem to come to grips with such closure. No more of this book nonsense, no more salty Alvin, just back to Monarch, yawn! What is wrong with me? Am I a madcap or something? No, I don't think so, but it's whatever. I guess all adventures have to come to an end at some point.

The next day was pretty customary. I returned to Monarch to work on more of my drivel. It was all back to the basics. Chris was blowing my email to smithereens, the Terror Twins running amuck, tormenting that poor intern Louise. Pretty boring stuff. At one moment, I felt my mind drifting away, wondering what Alvin actually does when he's asleep; the next, I kept thinking about hanging out with Darius. Between those various thoughts, I added stickers to my laptop, sharpened ten pencils, and drew one of those six-line cool "S" things from middle school. Any and everything to keep me off the topic at hand. That was at least until Garrett popped in.

"Hey, hey, Kiddo!" shouted Garrett, startling me in the middle of another one of my antics. *"Just got a text from Chris. He's wondering how the pre-edits are going?"*

I tried my best not to let my deadpan facial expression give my lack of progression away. But who in their right mind could blame me? I promise you six sentences into Trembly's book, and you'll be ready to use one of my over-sharpened pencils on your retina.

"Umm, edits are going great, Garrett! I think I'm finally finding my groove."

"Good to hear." Nodded Garrett. *"Remember it's me and you, kiddo?"* he said, brandishing his classic thumbs while taking a huge lap of his black coffee. *"Oh, and before I forget, I have a bit of a personal request. Don't feel obligated to agree either."*

Ugh, Garrett always gets me. How could I ever say no to him? He's like my dad away from dad, and he's always got my back. Yet, with a bit of hesitancy, I quickly blurted out, *"Umm...Sure, what's up?"*

Garrett let out a great sigh, breathing his coffee breath into the cool office air.

"The intern Louise, could you maybe, I don't know, take her out, get a few drinks or dinner with her, even a cup of coffee? I just feel so darn bad for her. Amber Lynn and Peyton have just been giving her the blues. You know how intense they can be. She's also new to

the city. Just show her the ropes. Is that cool with you?"

Geeze, how I really want to say no. But he's absolutely right. The Terror Twins, plus the pressures and stress of the Big Apple. Whew, I know that feeling. Besides, I guess I should at least attempt a normal social life, right?

"Yeah, that's fine with me." I shrugged.

"Awesome!" shouted Garrett. *"I knew I could count on you, homie."*

All I could do was smile and chuckle. Garrett's using slang always has a way of lifting my spirits. Speaking of spirits, I glanced through the glass office window only to see Louise getting badgered by Peyton. Talk about a dichotomy, and I couldn't in good conscience not do anything. Unfortunately, this little outing would have to wait at least a day or two. I need to get these edits done. Looks like work is having dinner with me again tonight. As I made haste to leave the building, I happily spat out those magic words just before hopping on my train.

"Tu et ego!"

"Yawn. Wow, that nap was just what the doctor ordered," said Alvin, as his voice finally came back into focus within my brain.

"So, how was the office today, madam?"

"Oh, the office was great, Alvin. Just a ball of fun and excitement. In fact, I can't think of any other place I'd rather be. Chris has somehow managed to become more annoying. I have to make a new friend with the new intern and best of all, I'm leagues away from completing my edits."

"Oh, that sounds amazing," joked Alvin, who is in much, much better spirits. Maybe he just needed a solid nap.

As we entered my apartment, I made a vow to dig my heels into this damn book. I whipped my phone out, ordered a pizza, and hopped to it. Crickets! Nothing but crickets, my pizza was nearly gone, and I had done nothing!

"I don't know Phoebe. Don't force it. You'll figure this out. Maybe you should just step back, take a hot shower, and decompress a bit," muttered Alvin in a caring tone. I love Alvin's sweet side. I'm glad it's back in the mix.

And as much as I hate admitting it, he's right. I need to just step away and give my brain a rest before jumping back in. Maybe even a little 20-minute snooze. Time to shut it down. I was defeated and worn out, and due for some quiet time. I whispered those words again, "*Tu et ego!*" and proceeded to nod off on the sofa.

During my slumber, I had a very strange dream. I was in the middle of a grassy park covered in bewitching Daffodils. It was warm but comfortable, and the sun was kissing my skin just right.

I slowly lifted my hand to the icy blue sky, only to have a large butterfly land on the tip of my finger. It tickled, flapping its brightly colored wings back and forth in perfect harmony before flying away. I felt drawn to its route and began to follow. Before I knew it, I was in a series of dark woods. The lush trees twisted and turned amongst one another, my bare feet crunching the forest compost with even the lightest of my strides.

Reaching the end of the dark trail, my eyes were forced to squint as a glowing green light bombarded them. My vision made an effort to adjust. I was able to make out a large glowing net of sorts. It was beautiful, yet intimidating. As I inched closer, I could hear a faint voice calling out, all before waking from my forty winks.

"What an odd dream..."

There I was, staring down the hallway of my better judgment, the gap between the stove and the counter calling my name. I had fallen asleep on the couch but awoke in front of my dingy stove. How did this happen? How did I get here? I knew that I shouldn't, but I couldn't resist. Looking at the buffet doesn't mean you have to eat it, right? I did my best to limit any noise within my apartment as if I would somehow wake Alvin. I'm such an idiot. Alvin is offline at the moment. It's just me and possibly a bad decision. Grabbing my phone from the countertop, I dropped to my knees and flashed my light between the gaps, reaching back for the text.

What was I doing? I knew the danger but didn't seem to care. It was like something was taking over me, or at least acting as a copilot. Rising to my feet, I placed the dish towel on my cluttered counter, pushing aside various snacks, old receipts, and work documents. The Night Script was revealed as I folded back the now dust bunny-covered towel. My hands began to shake as I unbuckled the book's rusty straps.

"God, one little cut from these bad boys, and I'm gonna need a tetanus shot."

Sifting through the old, worn pages, each rubbing between my index and thumb tip offering the same friction of a match and a lighting strip, I was in awe. This text was old, definitely Latin, which I was somewhat familiar with but not fluent in. But the pages, I tell you, the pages! Pure works of art, like a Henry Fuseli sketch or something.

It was all too intriguing, covered from top to bottom in scribbles, pictures, symbols, monograms, pentagrams, and various paganistic symbols. As I combed through the book, I noticed various words that jumped out to me, most being the basics: *ignis enchant, aqua spellan, lucendi micare*. But the one that really caught my to-and-fro eyes was '*augendae mentis,*' or Enhance Mind. I wonder what that could possibly do. I lifted the book to the front of my face and began to rattle off the words to the best of my ability. Reaching the end of my incantation, I waited for that defining moment of sorcery, pointing my twisted fingers like some Dr. Strange wanna-be. Nothing! Just the clickety-clack of my radiator.

"What a joke! Where's the bang? Where's the flash? No smoke, no fog? At least give me a magical beast or genie?"

Deep down, I was a bit relieved at the dud. And yet, I couldn't help but feel a bit duped by Alvin, chalking it up to him being overly paranoid. As I began to lurch back to my sunken sofa, a minor headache struck. I could feel my eyes letting in more light than usual. It felt like someone had added a larger aperture setting to my optics, *"sniff, sniff."* The neighbors are cooking four floors up, chicken tikka masala, it seems. All of a sudden, I remembered where I had placed my retainer five days ago and noticed every speck of dust lingering in my apartment. My brain was on overdrive. It was like being on Dexedrine but to the 10th power.

My mind was clear, crystal clear. I immediately grabbed Trembly's tell-all, popped the cap off of my red pen like a champagne cork, and went to town. The tell-all was complete trash, but I was in the zone; corrections here, comments there, I was on fire! With my nose buried in the work, I easily crushed the assignment in a matter of what seemed like minutes. My hair was in a frizz, panting as if I had just run 10k.

"Wow, that was insane. Just...wow!"

I paused to look down upon my accomplishment, seemingly snapping back to my current reality. If the *Night Script* had this kind of power, what else could it do?

"No, no, no, no, no, absolutely not! Phoebe, this was a one-and-done!" I shouted.

My next reaction was surely the correct one as I slammed the *Night Script* closed and slid it back into its hiding spot. Now, sitting on the couch, still in disbelief, I came to the realization that I needed to vent about what had just occurred, but to whom? Definitely not Alvin, and I don't want Garrett to think that I'm crazy. I do want to keep my job. So, what's a girl to do?

"I've got it! I'll call Darius." Besides, it was still kinda early in the night, and this was the perfect excuse to slip in a date. Without hesitation, I picked up my phone and sent a text.

"Hey stranger, what are you up to?" Send.

I began to bite my nails in nervousness. Hopefully, he replies. Gasp…. He was typing, biting my lip as the four little typing indicators danced across my screen.

"Sure, what's the plan?" read his response.

I could barely contain my excitement upon reading it. The problem is I don't know what I was truly excited about. Having a date with this amazing guy and possibly driving him away by opening up about everything that's going on with me? Or maybe it was the fact that I totally roasted Trembly's tell-all and was going to score major points with Garrett and Chris. I was also a tad nervous about Alvin. I felt like I was cheating on him. Or what if he finds out what I had done, along with the consequences that may come with it? Whichever one it was, one thing was blatantly obvious to me: I wanted to know what else the *Night Script* had to offer. It's almost as if it's calling my name.

Chapter Four
Cabbage white

As I finished my makeup and hair. It was finally time for my date with Darius if you can call it a date, that is. We decided on something small and low-key. There was a great little hipster bar near my place, and I promised tacos. We could grab a table, get some drinks, and just gel. Yeah… gel, who the hell am I kidding? There's no good way to say, *"Hey, by the way, I have another person in my head, and I own a spell book."*

This is going to go bad. Maybe I just don't mention it. But the guilt is kinda getting to me. It's bad enough that I completely went against Alvin's word. So, I need to get off on the right foot this time. If he truly likes me, he'll hear me out. After a lifetime of getting ready, outfit after outfit, shoe after shoe, I finally pulled it off. Not too skanky and not too reserved. Just have to grab my keys and get a move on.

When I entered the kitchen to retrieve them, my eyes drifted to the stove. Temptation is real, and maybe I should take the book with me. It's probably safer than here all by itself. No, no, this isn't right. What was I thinking? Leave the book where it is. Yet, no matter how much I resisted, it seemed to lure me in. I quickly snatched it up and tossed it in my purse, pivoting my direction to that of the stairs. Just as my foot hit the first step, my head began to spin, my eyes tightened to a squint, and my vision went in and out of focus. I shook my head, rattling it back to normal.

"That's odd. Probably should get some Tylenol or something. I'll stop at the corner store."

After a few blocks of walking and chugging a bottle of water, the headache slowly dissipated, and I was now at my destination. Okay, deep breaths. It's cool, just be yourself. No, I can't do this. I think I should bail. Yet, just as I turned to leave, a familiar voice rang out.

"Pajamas! What up, what up. Glad to see you made it out."

There he was, smack dead in front of me, bright smile and all. Welp, no turning back now.

"Well, if it isn't Monsieur Darius. Oh Darius, sweet Darius, could you be so kind?" I joked in a fake British accent.

"Ha, so you got jokes, huh."

"Hey man, just trying to keep up. I love this bar. P.S., shall we head in?"

Darius and I found a nice table in the corner of the mildly crowded bar. It was odd. I had never seen him outside of his uniform. He wore a tan bomber jacket and black jeans with a deep red t-shirt underneath. His brown skin blended perfectly with his color pallet. He was oddly smooth. Something about his swagger just screamed cool. He had the same confidence as Alvin but in a different way. When Alvin had a body, he was preppy, but Darius was chill and relaxed. He raised his right hand, sending an air gesture to the waitress to come over. I could see even the waitress was swooning over him. Maybe I was a bit out of my league again.

"So, what will it be for you?"

"Oh, umm, me?"

"You're the only other person at this table, pajamas," laughed Darius.

"Right, umm, I'll just have a Jack and Coke."

"So what made you finally reach out? I gotta be honest. I didn't think you would."

And he wouldn't be wrong, but I'm not really sure what's been going on with me. I've never been the bold type. Darius fiddled with the salt shaker, anticipating my response.

"Not sure. I managed to catch up on all of my work and feed my cat, and the night was still young. So, with that being said, I thought, 'gee Phoebe, why not give that goofy Darius guy a call.'"

Darius let out a cute little chuckle. It was nice to see the emotions of the guy I was into for a change.

"So, what made you message back?"

"Well, if I'm being totally honest, you have a good personality, you like to joke, and you're pretty cute. So, I figured with 8 million people in a city, I shouldn't pass a potentially good thing up."

Before I knew it, the bar had filled up with a slew of New Yorkers. Darius and I had been talking for hours, but it felt so natural. I felt like an entirely different person. Melted away was the wall, the wall of shyness, the wall of lack of confidence. All of my thoughts seemed to be on the table. Minus my enormous elephant in the room. I learned a lot about him. He was into football, his favorite team being the Steelers. He loves candy, particularly those sour watermelon-like slices, and Red Vines. He went to college for Computer Cloud engineering but had to drop out due to his mother's health, hence his working as a concierge. It was time. Now was the best chance I was going to get to spill the beans. With one last exhale, I started to speak, but he beat me to the next word.

"Do you believe in the supernatural?"

What a perfect segue! But it's best to play it safe.

"You mean like ghosts and stuff? Yeah, I guess I do, to a degree. I mean, something in this world just can't seem to be explained. One minute you're here, then you're gone. Where do we go when it's over, ya know? Our world, our very existence, is all so strange, right?"

"Exactly!" shouted Darius with a bit of tipsy in his voice.

This was my chance. Just jump into it. But yet again, Darius beat me to it.

"See, my mother, when she first became sick, she was only given six months to live. Just six months! But time and time again, her time was extended. Every chemo appointment, she fought and bounced back. There has to be something out there, just something. The doctors were baffled. Then, one day, she was cleared. She's still weak and needs my help, but she beat it. That's not luck, that's, I don't know, something else at play."

I was speechless; it just goes to show that you never really know what someone is dealing with. Pure sadness existed in his eyes. I guess this truly wasn't the best time. I had to lighten the mood a bit, so I placed my hand on top of Darius.

"Hey, do you want to hit the dance floor?"

Darius let out a tiny laugh, *"Guess I killed the mood a bit, huh?"*

"Not at all!"

I took his hand and guided him to the floor. It was an early 2000s night. We danced to all the classics, laughing at my lack of rhythm, but we didn't care. It was like we were all alone on the floor, one left foot in front of the other, eventually tripping on my own heels and landing in his arms. I wish I could say we had that magical movie moment and shared a kiss. Alas, that wasn't the case. The headaches were returning, this one being far worse than earlier. What the heck was going on? I needed some air.

Darius helped me make my way to the front of the bar, sitting me on a stoop to gather myself.

"You okay?"

"Yeah, I've just been getting these odd headaches as of late."

"Well, maybe we should just call it a night and get you home," he smiled, brushing my messy hair out of the corner of my eye. The night was still so early, but perhaps he was right. I pulled myself up, brushed my clothes clean, and began returning to my apartment. We strolled block after block, chatting it up as my headache slowly faded.

"How are you feeling?"

"Better, much better. It's like my brain is finally coming back together. Guess that's what they call a splitting headache."

With those very words, I finally realized what was happening to me. Alvin! He's been dormant for too long, and it's affecting my psyche. I have to wake him up, or who knows what will happen. It's now or never. If I'm going to tell Darius what's going on, I should do it quickly.

"Hey, Darius, can I tell you something? And… Please try not to judge me, no matter how odd it seems."

Darius smiled, spinning the brim of his hat in reverse. *"Sure, I kinda owe you one after killing the vibe earlier."*

"Okay, well, here it goes." My deep exhalation could be seen in the winter's wind. I couldn't believe I was finally about to open up to another person. My wall is down. Let's hope this works.

"A few weeks ago, I died. Or at least I think I died. My life was cut short, and a guy by the name of Alvin tried to save me with magic. But he was too late, so he fused his life force with me, and now he's, ya know, kinda stuck in my head. I know this all sounds crazy, but there's also this spell book that belonged to a witch, maybe a devil, and I'm stuck in the middle of all of this mess."

Darius gave a stare, followed by a look of deep interest, *"Wow."*

"That sounds like a great story. You should put that on paper. Sci-fi is back in style. Just look at all of the comic book movies that keep popping up."

"No, Darius, I'm serious. This is not like that. This…this is real…and scary."

Darius moved in to offer a comforting hug, but I immediately backed away. I don't need hugs or some form of male pity. I need a freaking ear. I could tell he was picking up on my seriousness; whether he believed me or not is another story.

"So let me get this straight: you are possessed and unknowingly involved in some sort of witchcraft?"

A bit heavy on the description, but he's not wrong.

"Prove it?"

Prove it? What the heck is this? I don't owe anyone an explanation. However, I do need some buy-in right about now. So I obliged, but the question is how? I got it! The *Night Script*. I pulled the tattered book from my purse, showing it to Darius. I could see the wonder, confusion, and curiosity in his eyes as he turned the stale pages.

"This thing is old, and what is this language that it's written in Latin? Wow, Pheebs, this is incredible. Do you know how to read this?"

A side of me felt cocky as I shrugged my shoulders with a nod of approval. *"Well, some of it I can read. But other parts are in an entirely different language that I don't know."*

Now that I had his attention, Darius agreed to hear me out, so we stopped at a local coffee shop so I could explain it all.

"Wow! Pajamas, this is heavy. If this book is this powerful, think of what you could do!"

I placed my hands over my face in frustration. His excitement is affecting his hearing.

"Weren't you listening, Alvin said we can't. If I do, we run the risk of releasing that Devil thingy."

"Okay, so what!" Darius quickly fired. *"What if he's just saying that to scare you, keep you in check? What if he just doesn't want you to have power or the life that he had? Who knows? I mean, you were dead. What really happened? Is he telling you the truth? A guy doesn't get by that long without secrets. Besides,*

how do you even know if any of these spells work? It could be all cap."

"No, not all of it. I did manage to cast one spell before."

But what if Darius is right? Maybe I really don't know Alvin, his intentions, or anything but bits and pieces of his past. Maybe I just got so caught up in his allure that I forgot to do my own research. Is he using me for something, too?

"Maybe you're right. You're right. You know what, Darius? Let's test this Night Script out! A few more small incantations can't hurt. Let's see, hmm."

We sat at the cafe table, combing through the *Night Script,* looking for something that I could decipher. Three coffee cups were in, and I finally found it.

"Look at this one, Darius. By the way, I never asked, "Do you prefer Darius, or is there a nickname I should call you?"

Darius gave a cheeky grin, *"My friends all call me Superman."*

I couldn't help but let out a geeky snort of a chuckle. *"Is that so?"*

*"Naw, Darius works just fine," h*e shrugged.

"Fine, Superman, look at this spell here. It reads, 'Tertius oculus meus est fidelis. Movebit te.'"

"What the heck does that mean?"

"Well, simply put, it means, 'My third eye will move you.' or something along those lines."

"Cool…so I guess with this spell, you can move things with your mind. Kinda like telekinesis?"

"I guess we'll find out."

In my mind, the spell just sounded cool. So why not try it? I have no idea what it actually does, but

Darius was right. Why not try? Was I really truly ready to commit my entire life to Alvin's rules? I placed the book in front of my face and gestured my hand with twisted fingers, focusing on the sugar jar at our table. *"Tertius oculus meus est fidelis Movebit te."* Again, no bang, no flash, not even a gust of table sugar. Darius and I stared at the jar, waiting for it to rumble, shake, or even tip. But before we could fully analyze, a waiter was standing by our table holding two lattes.

"Um, I'm sorry we didn't order these."

"Yeah, I don't think...."

Something was off here. The waiter was silent, almost mannequin in nature. We stood up from our seats to examine the odd gentleman, waving our hands over his glossy, lifeless eyes. He seemed normal enough, definitely breathing, but upon further inspection, his eyes were glowing a faint green.

"Wait, this was the spell!" I shouted! *"This spell doesn't move objects. It moves people."*

Darius removed the lattes from the waiter's zombie-like hands and placed them on the table. The waiter snapped back to normal, seemingly unaware of the events that just took place. But how did I do it?

"I wanted another latte, sure, but... Wait...That's it. The spell uses my wants to control a person's movements."

I could feel it in my bones. This was definitely how the spell worked. I knew the effects didn't last long, as the waiter was already helping another table, but what a rush this was! Darius and I must have been in sync with our thoughts because a night on the New York strip sounded like a splendid idea. Through the course of the night, multiple spells were cast for various forms of entertainment and mischief. Nothing was off the table: bar service, free Uber rides, and VIP access to nightclubs that neither of our pockets could afford. All free 99 thanks to this spell. What a night it was!

It was now five in the morning as Darius and I walked back to my place. I haven't had that much fun since my college days, carefree and zero stress. Not to mention, Darius was real, not some being stuck in my head.

"Hey, Pajamas, I gotta admit, this was a pretty dope night."

"Same. It was just what I needed: this Alvin stuff plus work. My mind was starting to feel like a 30-car pile-up."

We stood in front of my building, feeling the awkwardness build as the liquor had run its course. I knew exactly what I wanted, but did Darius get the hint? Maybe our night was just a friendship kind of thing. Before my next thought could filter through my mind, I was in his arms. It was our moment, that movie kiss. Just enough snow falling, standing on a stoop in the middle of the Big Apple. I was speechless, and I think Darius was as well.

"I'm sorry. I should have asked. We were just so close, like face to face, that I..."

"No, no. It was just right."

This time, I leaned in, and we continued. I pulled away seductively, biting my lower lip after our second round of kissing. I didn't want this moment to end.

"I guess I'll text you," cheesed Darius.

"Yeah, I'd like that."

He proceeded to walk down the steps, scooping two handfuls of the fresh snow and tossing it into the air like Lebron James before the big game. I couldn't help but smile. My gaze was fixated on him as he walked away. Maybe things were changing for me after all. I felt brand new walking up the steps to my apartment. This little corner of the city no longer felt so small. I was happy. Yeah, happy, but why are my hands shaking? I was struggling just to get the key into my door, and the headache was coming back with a vengeance. Thump, Thump, Thump! My skull was on fire, and as my body became weak and unbalanced, it felt as if my blood sugar was dropping. I knew exactly what was going on. I had to summon Alvin back. My mouth was drying out, and the room was coming to a twirl. Ahh, say it stupid, say it, *Tu et ego.*

Thump…

"Phoebe, Phoebe."

I could hear Alvin's voice. He was back.

"Hey…Hey Phoebe, how long have I been gone? Are you okay? Can you move?"

It seems as if I passed out on the floor of my apartment. I wasn't sure of how long, and Sith was brushing my cheek, purring loudly. I felt as if I had slept for 12 hours, and my body felt better. Guess Alvin was telling the truth about that part. Our psyches are one, and speaking of truths, I have the feeling many of them were about to come out. As I lay sprawled across the floor, I spotted the *Night Script* scattered amongst the other thousands of items inside of my purse. And if I could see it, that meant Alvin could too. It was far too late to hide the book.

"Phoebe… Is that what I think it is? What is that book doing out? I thought we agreed to keep it in hiding. What did you do?"

"Wait, I can explain," I exclaimed, shuffling up my belongings before quickly clutching the book! Then it hit me: why do I have to explain? He should be explaining to me.

"On second thought, yeah, it's exactly what it looks like. I wanted to see what this book was all about!"

"Excuse me? Are you insane?" rang Alvin's voice. *"Did you not listen to anything I've warned you about? This is reckless and extremely dangerous. I can't believe you would go behind my back like this. I want an answer. I deserve an answer! Why?"*

I was tired of keeping my mouth shut. I wanted answers, too. Darius was right. What did I really know about Alvin?

"No, I'm the one who deserves answers!" My outburst stopped Alvin's rant cold. I wasn't sure who this new me was, but she had a backbone. She was intense and fearless, and I liked it. I pulled myself to my feet, staggered to my bathroom, and hunched over the sink. As I looked in the mirror to argue with Alvin, my eyes were beet red with anger and tears.

"I want answers! Hum, because you seem to keep a lot from me."

"I've told you everything. What else is there to know about Phoebe?"

"A lot! Like, who are you really? I can't shake the suspension that you're leaving things out. How do I

know if everything you've told me is true? Or how about that picture, hum? What was that about? Why is everything so secretive? In fact, I don't even know why you saved me in the subway that day. You barely knew me. Why make that sacrifice for a total stranger? And now, now we're bonded together forever. Something is not right, Alvin! A guy doesn't get by this long without secrets."

Alvin stood quiet in the mirror's void, feeling as if hours had passed before he would give a response. *"Secrets, huh."*

Raising his right hand, a large glass pyramid full of light appeared above his palm.

"You're right. I left things out, and you deserve to know. This isn't going to work if you can't trust me. I'll show you."

Chapter Five

Vanoort's crow

H mph, seeing is believing, I suppose, but these days, I'm not quite sure of anything I see, let alone what I should believe in. But whatever, Alvin was preparing to show me what seemed to be his honest truth. Within the pyramid, a baleful glow filled its glass casing; the fog inside the structure was twisting and turning, and I was captivated, thrown into a reverie. The world around me was not my own. It felt as if I were watching a play within the confines of another's mind. The stage was set, and so began the prologue.

In the 1700s, the idea of witchcraft was often feared and misunderstood. Many people believed that witches were evil, devil-worshiping individuals who used their powers for malevolent purposes. The truth, however, was much more complicated for some.

In a small village nestled in the rolling hills of what would now be considered Massachusetts, there lived two alluring sisters, Amelia and Caroline Wilson. The sisters often faced persecution and jealousy within their village walls. For though they were poor, many suitors sought their hands in marriage. In an attempt to expunge previous gambling debts, the father of the duo arranged for the women to be wed. You see, in the 1700s, marriage was often considered more of a political or financial arrangement than a romantic one. Many young women were forced into marriages with men they did not love in order to secure favorable alliances or to improve their family's social standing. As for Amelia and Caroline, they had but one weakness: the love for their father.

Happily, ever after, that's the great lie. The noblemen who swore to love them would soon become cold. They were notorious throughout the village for not only their deep pockets but also their drunken, barbaric, womanizing nature, discarding women like a sour child bored of a toy. Amelia and Caroline would often find themselves on the wrong end of haymakers, masking the pain with lies of accidents and convenient mishaps. Even their very own father, who was well aware of the abuse, turned a blind eye, all for the sake of his investments. Yet, even in these dark times, the two had each other.

As morning sunrise came and went, Caroline would often find herself seduced by the most vivid of dreams each night. She was lost in the brush of overgrown grass covered with butter-yellow Daffodils peppered throughout the motif. It was a great relief, feeling the warm rays of the sun, highlighting her pale skin. Such an empty void it was beautiful, yet lonely. Raising her hand to the blue sky above in hopes that she may swirl its colors like paint upon a canvas, a large butterfly made its way to the tip of her finger. Its fuzzy legs began to jog across her index with its brightly colored wings flapping gently back and forth before flying away.

Feeling drawn to its route, Caroline began to follow. Gone was the grassy field, replaced with a brushstroke of dark woods. The lush trees contorted amongst one another, with the crust of dead foliage slipping between her toes. Reaching the end of the trail, Caroline couldn't help but notice a humming green light. Behind the glow, a great net stretched between branches. Beautifully constructed with the precision of a seamstress. As she approached the net, a faint voice could be heard, only for Caroline to awaken to the cold winter's winds and hands of her abuser. Reality is brutal and unforgiving in its truths. But this would soon change.

On the evening of the Great Reaping of Samhain, Caroline was sent on an errand to collect tender in the local woods. She didn't mind such a task, which gave her time away from her husband's clutches. Typically, Caroline would invite her sister to catch up on the day-to-day banter, but it was clear from the bruises under Amelia's eye socket that she was not allowed to leave her duties at that moment.

But even within their duties, the duo managed to find a sense of mirth. One of Caroline and Amelia's guilty pleasures was their practice of Magic Circles. With such turmoil and chaos in their lives, protection magic was the only hope worth clinging to in spite of the stigmas and dangers it presented. Why not grab the necessary ingredients for a Kismet Star, one of Amelia's favorites?

As the sun began to set behind the trees, Caroline made her way through the dense forest, searching for ingredients. Father always told her to avoid going too deep into the woods, but curiosity always found a way to get the better of her. Draped in silence, the young woman noticed a strange rustling tightly knitted between the frost-bitten leafage. Caroline froze, listening intently, as her heart began to race.

To her surprise, a strange creature lay within the crunchy snow-covered pine needles. It was unlike anything Caroline had ever laid eyes on. A tall, muscular animal with the body of a man but the head of a Reynard. Its toned skin resembled freshly polished copper, with a set of large bat-like wings upon its back. Its only possession was a small, tattered pouch draped over its shoulder. Fear was the feeling that Caroline should have felt, but she was oddly at peace even as the creature set its gaze upon her.

"Who...art thou?" asked Caroline, testing the boundaries of her newfound bravery.

Turning its snout, the odd critter replied, *"I am a creature, not bound to this fiergen. I have spent all of an ecnes simply searching for my freedom. Yet, it seems my true fate was to make your acquaintance, Caroline,"* replied the creature in a deep, rumbling voice.

Caroline was taken aback. How did this creature know her name? His lips did not move, yet its voice rang clearly within her mind.

"How do you fare?" asked Caroline as the creature struggled to rise to its feet.

"Weary, I'm afraid. I fear my travels have taken a toll on me."

"You are the voice in my dreams, art thou not? The one beyond thy net."

"Perhaps a meal will restore thou strength." Caroline reached into her cloak and revealed two

large red apples. *"Tis not much, but it's better than nothing."*

The creature stared blankly at the fruit, studying its color and shape. Only to turn it away, placing it gently back in Caroline's hands.

"This nourishment will not suffice. I require something else if I am to return to my full strength."

Perplexed, Caroline placed the apples back into the pockets of her cloak. *"I can bring you something else. I'm a fairly decent cook. John even manages to stomach my meals."*

"Please understand, Caroline, the food of your world is inadequate for my kind. Only the dark rapacity of men satisfy my palate and bolster my strength. I have been seeking someone like you for a long time. Your rage is a thing of beauty. You're afraid, but not of me. You desire freedom as well as death, just as I do. The beatings, the punishment, all echo in the chambers of your soul? This world has been cruel to you and your sister, has it not?"

Caroline couldn't believe her ears. How did this creature know so much about her? Was it this obvious even to a stranger? Unknowingly, her hand raised to her cheek, a spot where the most recent bruise rested. What was this odd feeling? The creature was correct in his examination as her blood began to boil.

"I have a proposal for you if you are willing to accept it," said the creature in a suave tone.

Caroline hesitated, but her curiosity won out. *"Tell me, creature of the wood. What is thou bargain? I have but one request. Allow my sister into the fold."*

The creature reached into its pouch and produced a small glowing book. *"This is Night Script, imbued with the wisdom and knowledge of a thousand Devils. It will grant you power and focus beyond your years. Use the will of this text to obtain your freedom."*

Caroline reached out, swiftly snatching the book, savagely mesmerized by its ominous intensity. She could feel the warmth of its tattered jacket in her hand, the book's spine pulsating and beating with the might of a horse's heart. Her eyes sparkled with the intensity of the sun reflecting off morning lake water. Shifting from an earthy brown color to that of a deep sliver as she glossed over the text with sheer wonder.

"Thank you. I don't know how I could ever repay you. I didn't even gather your name."

The creature chuckled. *"I am called Gamigin, and there is no need for repayment. Simply use the Night Script, and it will benefit us both. In fact, allow me to accompany you back to your village,"* said *Gamigin* with a smirk.

"But you are far too weak to travel. Let me seek the aid of my sister. Perhaps we can carry you."

"That won't be necessary. Simply repeat after me, "*Tu et ego."*

"Tu...et...ego?" Caroline whispered the chant, feeling the cold wind rolling off her lips.

And with that, the creature vanished. Caroline stood alone in the woods, holding the *Night Script* in her cold hands. As she leafed through its pages, realizing that it was filled with dark, forbidden magic, a feeling of excitement and possibility washed over her. She knew that her life would never be the same, and she couldn't wait to tell Amelia. This was their chance. Her oppressors would feel every ounce of pain she had felt.

"Caroline, you must protect me. It is now your duty until my strength returns. I am you, and you are I."

Whispering *Gamigin* in the mind of the young woman, Caroline rushed back to the village, eager to tell her sister of her euphoric experience. Later that night, while their husbands were sleeping, the two sisters met deep within the woods to study the newfound text. At first, Amelia was hesitant to use the book, fearing the consequences of tampering with such powerful dark magic. But Caroline, curious and ambitious as ever, convinced her sister to try out a simple incantation. To their amazement, it worked, and they were able to conjure a small flame with ease.

Encouraged by their success, the sisters began to delve deeper into the book, practicing more and more advanced spells, all under the watchful eye and tutelage of *Gamigin*. The duo quickly discovered that they had a natural talent for dark magic, and before long, they were performing feats that even the most experienced Witches and Covens would have struggled to accomplish. As their powers grew, so too did their ambition. They began to dream of overthrowing their husbands and village, ruling as its queens, using their Devilic magic to bend the people to their will. And so it began, one conjure after the next, raining curses upon the unsuspecting. First on the list would be their husbands, both meeting their demise thanks to Black Magic in disguise as unfortunate accidents. Soon to follow would be their father's health, withering him away in the blink of an eye, quickly inheriting his fortunes and property.

The sisters were successful in their coup. They controlled their village with the fear of witchcraft, heavy purse strings, and Devilic suggestions to keep the people in line. But as the seasons passed, Amelia often found herself gazing out at the terrified faces of her fellow villagers; she realized that the cost of their power had been too high. They had sacrificed their morals and their humanity for the sake of their own ambition. Amelia became haunted by the guilt of what they had done, what they had become. She wanted out. But Caroline and Gamigin had other plans.

As the nights passed, Amelia found herself unable to rest easily. It was as plain as a pikestaff as to why. In order to ease her racing mind, she took to the porch for a bit of fresh air, and what she found, however, was Caroline venturing into the nearby woods. Normally, this behavior wouldn't seem strange, as the sisters would often study the *Night Script* within the tranquility of the brush, but never this late. Curious of the situation, Amelia gave pursuit. The woods were practically a different world under the cloak of darkness. It was a struggle to see so much as a hand in front of one's face, and there was no shortage of dangers along the way. Yet, Caroline seemed to have no issue navigating.

Making out shadows from a distance, Amelia noticed her sister's stride coming to a halt. Where exactly was she? In all her years, Amelia had never seen this section of woods. A large altar was brightly lit by flame. Vines covered a massive statue that resembled a fox. Caroline began to fixate her vision on a plot of dirt in front of her, dropping to her knees and beginning to chant. Entering into a zombie-like state, she reached into her pouch, removing a small bag of what appeared to be witch powder. The bones of fish with a dash of sage and lily dust. Caroline sprinkled a series of magic circles above the woodland soil. What was going on here? Amelia had seen many spells but nothing of this manner. Out of her sleeve, Caroline drew a larger dagger with the skull of an owl carved into its hilt. Raising her palm into the air, Caroline carved a large gash into her hand, spilling and squeezing her own blood into the center of the Magic Circle.

Within mere moments, the circle began to pop and sizzle, followed by a large cloud of purplish smoke and an amber light shot to the peaks of the snowy pines above. Amelia had never seen such magic. Lugubrious moans and groans drifted through the night's air. It's as if the souls bound to the forest were quivering in fear at the menacing presence within the swirling fog. The smog became thick, seeping into Amelia's lungs, forcing a cough as particles of dust flicked and whipped her face. The air began to clear as a tall, winged figure emerged.

It couldn't be…but Amelia's gut knew it to be true. This was Gamigin! She had never seen Gamigin with her own two eyes. She had only ever received descriptions from her sister or conversed with the creature's disembodied voice. But there was no mistaking it. This was him. The creature was translucent. She could see right through him, like the thin skin of an onion. He wasn't quite formed as of yet, but his power was immense. Caroline bowed at the feet of the creature, pledging her allegiance to the silent giant as he tested the dexterity within his fingertips.

Amelia backed away, covering her mouth, trying her best not to make a sound. What was going on here? Was her sister mad? Surely, she could feel the power percolating through the very flesh of this beast. How could she ever hope to control such a thing? Beads of sweat dripped down the ripples of her vertebrae. Her skin became clammy and pale, and she held back the urge to vomit. Amelia loved witchcraft as well as the power it bestowed upon her. But this...this creature was pure evil. Getting away was a top priority. If spotted, who knows what sort of danger she would be in? Blind and afraid, she darted through the black woods, hoping and praying that her route was true. Finally reaching the confines of their home, Amelia slammed the large red porch door behind her before curling into a ball and sobbing in the moonlight.

"You've made it back, sister."

Amelia quickly sat up, only to realize she was far from home. She was face-to-face with her sister and Gamigin.

"Is this it? Were they going to kill me?"

"Sister, allow me to introduce you to our master, Delegate of the Trionfi. He is the Naberius of the Seraphim bound to Solomon. Kneel before his suzerain, Gamigin."

Frozen with fear, Amelia knew this was not her sister but the power of Gamigin and the bond he possessed with her. The Devil towered over Caroline's shoulder, silent yet intimidating. Amelia knew she was in over her head, but how did this happen? How did such a creature …?

"Gain his sovereignty," interrupted Gamigin.

"I am you, and you are I. These were more than just mere words. Tis an oath. Your sister desired power, so I simply obliged. Freedom, wealth, beauty, all vain desires, nourishment to my body. Thou and Thie's sister were both slaves to avaricious natures. Those natures give life power to my body, followers to my cause, and food to my genus. Thy village is but a fragment of dust. In the grand scheme, this world is full of selfish hearts and wills. Plentiful nourishment. I shall use this flaw to tear open that which separates my Section from I. That cursed net, stitched by the hand of God, finally cut, freeing my brothers and sisters so they too may partake in the feast of humanity."

Always quick-witted, Amelia pretended to agree with the Devil. She was biding her time so that she may free her sister and somehow stop this nefarious plot. As the days passed, Amelia studied Caroline's witchcraft more intently. She learned spells far out of her range of ability. She knew stopping Gamigin would be a tall task, but she had to find a way, and her answers lay within the Night Script. Just one problem: the book never left her sister's side, so how would she possibly obtain it?

Fortune, however, has a funny sense of humor. One morning, whilst Caroline was away to the privy, the spell book lay unattended amongst her bed. With the opportunity in sight, it was finally time to implement the plan. Careful not to squeak on the dry wooden floors, Amelia's bare toes trickled across the hallway,

81

joining the two rooms. She had to act fast, stealing the book and making a break for safety in the confines of the mansion's basement. There must be something in here on how to stop Gamigin, but time was wearing thin, and if Caroline were to find out, she would surely kill her. Pushing aside a series of loose stones and crusty soil, Amelia hid the Night Script within the damp cellar. But how much time would this actually take? That's when an idea struck: stage the scene. Make it look as if the book had been stolen! Breaking the upstairs window and then proceeding into the wilderness, Amelia convinced herself to be oblivious. However, the loud shrill followed by a flock of fleeing crows simply reinforced her paranoia.

A sharp pain shot through Amelia's skull. It was Caroline communicating with her telepathically.

"Sister, the Night Script, it's gone!"

Playing along with the ruse, Amelia replied with a hint of concern, *"Missing! You jest, sister! What do you mean missing?"*

"Exactly as it sounds, you fool, the Night Script has been pillaged! The window of the house has been fractured. It must be one of the villagers revolting. They will die for this! Where art thou? Return here at once. We have much work to do."

As Amelia returned to her home, it was clear that Caroline had begun her onslaught. Several homes within the village had been set ablaze. The stench of burning straw and flesh wafted through the night. Droves of villagers gathered outside of the estate, all of them up in arms, tired of the oppression brought forth by us witches. What had she done? What have I done, pondered Amelia? Was her sister going mad?

No, this was Gamigin unleashing his rage, using her dear sister as a vessel.

This was the final straw. Within a blanket of anger and confusion, Amelia managed to slip into the basement by way of a candle, unearthing the Night Script. She shifted through the text with haste, hoping she would soon find a solution to her problem. This was a dead end. Frustrated and defeated, Amelia tossed the Night Script across the damp basement in a fit of rage. But, it would seem fate would decide to intervene once more. There it was, reflecting within a small puddle of stale water, gracefully lit by Amelia's candlelight, a spell that she had never laid eyes upon.

Crawling over to the book, Amelia inspected the text. So simple, yet so conducive, a "Lock and Key Spell." She may not be able to compete with Caroline and Gamigin, but she wouldn't have to. This spell could lock the creature away within the Night Script. It was not a difficult spell, so to speak, but her execution would have to be precise as the spell would extract Gamigin directly from her sister's being. Making her way to Caroline, Amelia couldn't help but feel an eerie presence within the estate. Gamigin must be physically manifesting. It's all starting to make sense. Caroline once mentioned that Gamigin does not eat food like us. Only the heinous avariciousness of men satisfy its appetite. Caroline and the villagers were all clueless about their deeds, anger, and hate, just pure nourishment.

Time was of the essence. Amelia made her way through the twists and turns of the manor before spotting Caroline along with a nearly formed Gamigin laying siege to opposing villagers from the foot of the porch. She could feel her grip tightening around the Night Script. This was the moment of truth, and the bit of honor she had left wouldn't allow for an ambush.

"Caroline, stop this lunacy!"

Caroline and the towering Gamigin turned to Amelia's direction, only to see her holding the *Night Script* close to her chest.

"You! Twas you! Thou art the traitor? Stealing that which does not belong to you. How could you? I demand the Night Scripts return this instant."

"It would seem you have a wish to visit Hell far sooner than intended. Tis not a fight you could win, for I am near completion. You will soon kneel before your Masters. As this world will soon be a haven for my brothers," whispered Gamigin within the confines of Amelia's mind.

Amelia could see an image forming in her head: ten Devils roaming the earth. Gamigin and his brothers enslaved humanity, feeding off of despair, sorrow, and greed. If this were to be true, she could not idly stand by.

"No," said Amelia with a soft sotto voice.

"No!" Her voice boomed with the second reply.

"Tis wrong sister, tis not you! I blame the creature. Its' terror stops here."

Amelia flipped open the *Night Script,* cupping the book's spine tight within her palm while raising her left swiftly into the air.

"Hafanti de galam sol ifrin. En vol shin nel gate nel chain."

A bright beam of green light shot out of the book as it hovered in the air. The creature was stronger than any man or beast Amelia had ever faced. Gamigin was able to resist the whirlpool of wind attempting to pull him into the pages of the book. But, more problems seemed to be surfacing as a struggle between herself and Caroline ensued. Caroline drew her dagger, slashing the wrist of Amelia. Blood was flowing quickly, oozing down Amelia's forearm, but Amelia was clever and resourceful. She remembered her training in spell-casting, spewing a stream of fire to heat Caroline's blade to a scorching orange glow in the palm of her hand. With Caroline temporarily immobilized, Amelia returned to carefully crafting the spell, drawing the monster's body into the pages of the book.

The Devil struggled as his resistance slowly dwindled against the magic. The tables were turning Gamigin. He scratched and clawed at the bezel of the book, but Amelia was more determined than ever, and with a flash of light, the Devil was trapped. Falling to her knees, weary from the struggle, Amelia smiled as she closed the spell book with a slam. But, the victory came with a price. On one hand, the Devil would never harm anyone again. However, something was wrong. It was Caroline. There she was, lying amongst the devastation caused by the entrapment of Gamigin. A beam of wood crushed her fragile sternum. Amelia tried lifting the beam but was far too weak and, unfortunately, drained of any magic.

"Sister, can you hear me? Please hold on. I can retrieve aid," cried Amelia.

The remaining villagers watched from a distance. None willing to help.

"Are you all so cruel? Help me move this, please, please HELP!" screamed Amelia.

"Amelia..." whispered Caroline.

"Thank you for freeing me from that Devil. Tis not what I wanted for my fate, yet his grip was far too powerful. Many a night, I could feel myself crying out to you, only to have his evil cover my mouth and pull me back into the void. I did not want this. But I knew you would hear me all along."

Caroline placed her fading hand upon her sister's cheek. The contrast between the warmth of the living and the cold of the dying is evidently clear.

"Sister, he has stopped for now. But such a spell will not hold forever. I learned a lot whilst being his host."

Pulling Amelia close, Caroline began to whisper.

"Tis only one way to end his terror. The Night Script cannot be destroyed. No spell can truly bind him. Gamigin's true name, utter it, the power of names, a Devil's true fragility. Utter his name... Ten Devils wait at the net, seeking sustenance.... Utter his true name and send him back. Find Belphegor, *as he may know the way."*

Silently, the secret between the two sisters was exchanged, but what it meant was a mystery just before dying in Amelia's arms. The room went cold as if all of the evil winds had been filtered out. Caroline lay still with her eyes wide open. They say only those who are truly wicked lose the pleasure of seeing the darkness of their own eyelids upon death. Amelia's tears dripped down her sister's cheek as the morning sun kissed the scorched earth before her.

As the months passed, Caroline had been given a proper witch's burial, and the fortune of the two was solely inherited by Amelia. As for the *Night Script*, Amelia took the book deep into the dark woods, ripping the page containing Gamigin 's seal out. She knew destroying the page was not possible. But that wasn't part of the plan. Amelia dug deep into the surface of the earth, covering the page with the rich new spring soil. Opening her cloak, Caroline's dagger was drawn. Amelia studied the knife before plunging its dull edge into the stale trunk of a tree.

"Let the future correct our sister's failure. For now, the beast sleeps. But when his slumber ends, may the power of this name burn his flesh and lock him forever in Hell," she murmured.

Exiting the woodlands, a large stagecoach sat idle, waiting for her arrival. The reinsman loaded the carriage with her belongings.

"All is ready, M'lady."

Taking one last whiff of the spring wind, she boarded the wagon, making her way to New York City to begin her new life. This chapter was coming to a close, all of her evil deeds buried with Caroline and the pages containing the Lock and Key spell.

In lieu of her new life, Amelia became Allison. It wouldn't take long for Allison to adjust. Using the money from her inheritance, she purchased a house in the middle of the city. With witchcraft in the rearview, perhaps it was time for a new passion. The city was full of life. It was refreshing and ripe with opportunity. Why not own a few pieces of the soon-to-be Big Apple? With that in mind, Allison became one of the few women to take up real estate law. Quickly becoming a star in her field and one of the only females taken seriously at the time, she was striking deals with some of New York's most elite families and socialites.

That's when she met him, Thomas Casen. Allison was independent and hadn't required a man's presence since the killing of her first husband, but that was in the past. Thomas was different. He was a gentleman and would die before raising his fist at her. His charisma and charm could light the darkest of banquet halls. Conversation was effortless and easy with Thomas, and his knowledge of architecture was unmatched. They hit it off instantly, viewing each other as equals, which was seen as odd at the time. The two became what modern times would consider a power couple in the real estate world. But real estate would become the duo's second joy, with the birth of their son being the first.

That son was me, Alvin Casen. The boy who would grow up with a love for literature, not land. I wish I could take back all of the things I've said. One evening, while rummaging through a pile of dusty books in the cellar, I came across one journal and another thing that was something far stranger. I discovered my mother's past. An aunt she never mentioned, murder, magic, and, worst of all, witchcraft. I was furious at my findings! The hypocrisy! Mother preached the idea of good and honesty, but there is nothing honest about her in the slightest.

Though I was angry, I couldn't help but be inspired by what these tales had to offer. Mother warned me of the book's power. She told me it was not the inspiration I was feeling but the pull of the Night Script. I didn't listen. I was greedy and foolish and felt my mother couldn't be trusted, thanks to her checkered past. We had many disputes, yet before I could apologize, it was far too late. You can cry your woes at the foot of them all you like, but caskets won't talk back. A lesson I was learning all too well. It wouldn't be long before Father's passing. The love of his life had been extinguished. The heartbreak and pain snuffed out his once bright spirit.

Here, I was wealthy but empty. The only thing that was capable of curing my sadness was my writing, and the Night Script was more than willing to help. I wrote many books under my pseudonym. My creativity was at its highest, and nothing would take this from me, not even death. I used its magic to prolong my life, but something wasn't right. Yes, the Night Script granted my spell, but it began feeding on me the same. Gamigin was growing. I could feel his evil creeping under my skin. The more I used, the deeper into the void I drifted. I couldn't keep such a thing up in good conscience. It took every fiber of my being to abandon its powers.

For years, I've struggled with resisting the temptation of the Night Script, but I was always able to keep my urges at bay. That is until I realized my *Spell of life* was beginning to wear off. Selfishly, I wasn't ready to leave, and the power of the Night Script was beginning to call out again. In one small moment of weakness, the cursed book took control, infusing my hopes of extending my stay in this world. But a *Spell of life* can only be cast once per individual, an extension of 300 years, no longer. I was not myself. I searched the book for answers and counters, anything to stay alive. One spell after another, all seeming to be in vain.

That is until the night that I saw you die. Then it hit me, the *Melding Magic* spell. This was my chance. Sure, my body would go, but my essence would live on with you until I could find a way to restore my body. I know it was selfish, but I couldn't let Gamigin have all of me, and seeing you like that truly did break my heart. I am sorry. But this is my point. This book is dangerous. It changes you, and it manipulates your mind. Gamigin is pure poison. Feeding on your desires for his own benefit.

Alvin could see the disappointment on my face. He used me. In spite of what he says, this was never about saving me. This was just a self-absorbed tactic working to his advantage. I was speechless to the point of feeling ill. But what was I going to do? I was stuck with him.

"Phoebe, say something, anything."

I was frozen, heartbroken. This was a fate seemingly worse than death. Alvin used me, and I don't think I can ever forgive him.

Chapter Six
Common Brimstone

For the remainder of the morning, I tried to wrap my head around Alvin's lies. He had pleaded his case, only proving Darius' intuition to be spot on. I didn't know Alvin or his motives. He was using me. I would love to sit here and sell up the whole self-blame attitude. But screw that noise, he's the manipulator, and I owe him nothing. If saving my life was a means of simply saving his own, then I was better off dead.

"Seriously, Alvin, you're scum. No, you're worse than scum. And to think I... thought you were special or different. You bash your mother for being a liar and a monster, but the truth is you're no better. I guess it's in your blood. I actually feel sorry for you, all of these years of being helpless, conniving, and selfish. We may be stuck together, but I'm nothing like you. I'm not helpless, and I will never prey on another person just to benefit my own motives. Unlike you, I have people who will support me and my dreams. I pity you."

Alvin was silent in my head, but I could feel his mannerisms, the clenching of his jaw tight like a channel lock. He was angry but also sad. Was I being harsh? Maybe. But this is what he had coming.

"Do you have anything to say at all?"

I could feel him fixing his lips to reply, but my rage cut him off mid-sentence.

"On second thought, keep it to yourself. At this point, there is nothing you can say. We may share my mind, but make no mistake, we are done! As a matter of fact, it's way past my bedtime."

"Phoebe, please wait…"

"Nope, Tu et ego."

My mind was radio silent again, yet with no Alvin, my own personal thoughts were free to run rampant. Luckily, it was still the weekend, so there was no need to get up, so my curtains remained sealed to a blackout. Time at this point might as well have been a mannequin. I was super exhausted. Closing my eyes was the most logical thing to do, but all I could think about was how stupid I was for trusting him. This jerk ruined my magical night. I should have known better. Why didn't I do my research on him and this stupid book? Not too late, I suppose. Heck, if I'm going to be stuck with him for the rest of my life, I should probably find out all of his dirty laundry. Yeah, this seems like a smart play. I'm pretty far ahead with my work, and Monarch has access to a vast catalog of data that is not even accessible online. There's bound to be something out there on him. Alvin has met his match this time. First thing tomorrow, I'm hitting the archives, but I should really get some rest first.

As the morning sun peeked through the seam dividing my curtains, another day at the office loomed in the not-so-distant future. Unfortunately, I had to get the most annoying part of my Monday morning over with.

"Ugh, here goes nothing…Tu et ego."

"Finally," yawned Alvin.

"Good morning, Phoebe."

I placed my hand over my eyes as I brushed my teeth. The last thing I wanted to see was this jerk's reflection. It's bad enough that I had to hear his annoying, whiny voice so early in the morning. After dropping my toothbrush into its cup, I turned the sink's hot water to full blast, banking on the steam to block out Alvin's image.

"Phoebe, this is ridiculous. Hear me out, please. I'm sorry!"

I couldn't help but spew out a sarcastic chuckle while spitting out a glob of greenish toothpaste.

"Sorry, you're sorry? No, you're a user and a liar. That's what you are!"

"Phoebe, I'm telling you, I wasn't myself…"

"Let me take a crack at it, Alvin. The Night Script is an old, trusty, evil Night Script. That's what you were going to say, right? Let me guess, it controlled you? Tell me, Alvin, the Night Script preys on what?"

The fog on the mirror was slowly disappearing, and I could now see Alvin holding his hands over his mouth and nose in a frustrated, prayer-like manner.

"Well… say something."

Alvin placed his hands in the pockets of his navy blazer, looking up to the infinite void of rolling fog and white steam.

"It preys on a person's wants and desires, Phoebe."

"Exactly! Keyword wants, Al, YOUR wants."

I proceed to continue my morning routine, my frustrations at level ten. Of course, in the process, I managed to overflow my coffee mug, drop my laptop, and forget where I placed my keys and metro card. Needless to say, I was off to an amazing start.

Everything that could go wrong this morning would. I hate to admit it, but this drama with Alvin was getting to my head. I was so zoned out this morning that I even missed my train, and it was literally right in front of me, but in spite of my missteps, I managed to make it to Monarch with two minutes to spare.

"Phoebe, can I please just say one thing?"

"I thought we had this conversation already, Al. I don't care. Now, leave me alone. Some of us have to work today."

"Tu et ego."

As I scampered into my office, everything seemed to be at ease at Monarch for a change, and thanks to the Night Script, I was well ahead of my work. Plopping down into my ergonomically friendly chair, I twisted my arms like a Nathan's Pretzel and cracked my knuckles above my head. Time to do some detective work. I scoured file after file for hours but couldn't find a single thing about Alvin. Not an article, short story, journal, nada. I knew he was a liar. He probably made up that writer stuff just to lure me into his twisted little world. But what about the Night Script? It's old, but maybe there is a mention of it somewhere. Again, another dead end. I was striking out hard today.

"Something's gotta give," I snarled, slamming the Night Script to a close.

"Ring, ring, ring!"

What the, my office phone is ringing? It never rings. I didn't even know I had an office phone until about a month ago. Garrett usually calls my cell if he wants to reach me. What's the deal here? Picking up the ringer, my hand began to shake as if I were sprinkling salt. I was nervous. Maybe I was getting canned. This was my third call-off in under two months, after all.

"Phoebe Graham's office." I could feel the shakiness in my voice upon answering.

"Hi, Phoebe. It's Louise. I'm here at the front desk, and umm, you have a visitor here to see you. Shall I send 'em to your office or hold 'em here?"

"A visitor?" here at…Monarch. This couldn't be good.

"Umm, wait. No, keep whoever it is there. Does this person have a name? …. Hello? Hello?"

Crap, she hung up already. What was I going to do? I tried calling back. No answer. Should I call security? No, that will draw way too much attention. I guess I just have to pull up my bootstraps and figure it out. As I crept down the hall, I could make out a figure wearing a hoodie. Who was this mystery man? Needless to say, I was still a bit traumatized. Rightfully so, strangers haven't been the most trustworthy as of late. Within a few weeks, my emotions have been beaten senseless, from death to liars to love. But I pressed on.

"Umm, hello, how can I help you?" I mumbled.
"Help me."

The figure whipped around to reveal a bouquet of beautiful roses. It was Darius! I slapped my hands over my mouth as his towering stature wrapped his arms around me. I was speechless. This is possibly the most romantic thing any guy has ever done for me. Well, that's a bit of a shortlist. But even so, major points for him. I lifted my glasses to my forehead, swiping away my sappy tears, giving Darius the biggest squeeze, followed by a kiss. This guy was legit.

"What the heck are you doing here? I can't believe you right now," issuing a playful slap to his broad shoulder.

"This is just…God, are you a real person? Unbelievable," I swatted playfully.

"Good unbelievable or bad unbelievable? Ahh, who am I kidding? You love it. Admit it," joked Darius before planting another kiss on me.

"Can't a guy stop past to see his lady?"

His lady. He called me his lady. Are we like a thing?

"So, I'm your lady now?"

"I think so. That is, if you wanna be," smiled Darius.

I was officially head over heels. I clutched my roses close to my chest, giving them a deep whiff.

"Well, how about we get some dinner when I'm free from this palace and catch up? Just a guy and his lady, was it?"

Darius drew a crescent moon grin, showing off his marvelous smile.

"I think I can do that."

He reached out his hand, clutching mine, stretching our arms to an extended distance. I didn't want to let go, but I did have to get back to work. Releasing my palm, Darius faded away, slowly disappearing into the silver elevators. I lifted the roses to my nose and took another whiff.

"Wow, looks like you've got yourself a winner."

I turned to see Louise. She flashed a smile as I struggled to mask my giddy expression.

"Yeah, he's umm, something. I mean, it's new, but this feels different than anything before. It's only been a few minutes, and I already miss him to pieces."

"Psssh, you're one of the lucky ones," said Louise, gently biting on the back of her blue pen.

"I've been in this city my entire life and never had a single flower given to me. I'd say you're doing pretty well," with a sarcastic chuckle.

Hmm, I guess I am lucky, but how could a girl as pretty as Louise have such bad luck with men? That chuckle may have been sarcastic, and even though she was smiling I could tell she wanted something real and legit. She wanted her own Darius. Nothing wrong with that, but Garrett was right. I should show her a night out. Besides, I've been in her shoes before, and oddly enough, I see a bit of myself in her, so why not? I placed my roses gently on the desk in front of me and took a deep, silent breath.

"Hey Louise, if you're not busy Friday, would you like to go and maybe grab a drink or two after work? You know, a little girl's night out."

Louise's eyes lit up with excitement. She seemed to have been caught off guard.

"Umm, yeah, sure, definitely!" stumbling her words.

"Maybe you can give me a few guy tips," she joked.

I think I'm the last person qualified to give guy advice, but what the hell?

"Sure, I think I can do that. Friday it is. Well, I have to get back to the office. Hope your day goes well."

"Hey Phoebe, before you head back, can I ask you some…?"

It was in that moment of slight pause that life would change. I wish I could say for the better, but that stuff only exists in sappy fairy tales, you know, glass shoes and poisonous apples, clashes between good and evil.

So evil, what is it exactly? According to Merriam-Webster, evil is morally reprehensible: sinful and wicked. An evil impulse arising from actual or imputed bad character or conduct. A person of evil reputation. To my knowledge, the Night Script had a reputation for being evil, housing the allegedly most wicked creature within its pages. And unbeknownst to my knowledge, something within the walls of Monarch was being brewed.

At some point during my magical moment with Darius and feeling sorry for Louise, the luminous glow of the dark Night Script was radiant, its festering rage and evil feeding on the negative energy within the walls of Monarch. One giant glass cocoon, full of egos, ambitions, and cutthroat business.

Flipping itself open, the words began to glow brightly as the book started to shake and rattle, lifting itself into the air. The pages turned themselves as the words flew out of the book on the wings of a spooky groan. A powerful spell was recited, itself followed by a glowing trail of cosmic green light zipping and whipping throughout the halls, unnoticed to the untrained eye. As the spell book floated back down to the desk like a feather drifting in the wind, something was happening. I even missed it.

Louise sat quietly at her desk, pausing mid-sentence of our icebreaker of a conversation. Her eyes went blank as if she were daydreaming. I waved my hand in front of her square frames.

"Louise. Earth to Louise."

No response. How strange! Just a glassy-eyed stare fixated on an unknown spot.

"I would really appreciate it if you kept your hand out of my face!" Snapped Louise.

Louise had suddenly become agitated and angry for no reason, and that was just the tip of the anger iceberg.

"I'm so sorry. I was, I was just joking. Is…everything okay?"

The colleagues in proximity began to stare with concern, but it was evidently obvious no one wanted to be on the end of this rope.

"Everything's just fine...Phoebe. If you don't mind, I have a lot of work to do, and I don't require any further distractions."

Louise's vision quickly diverged from my eyes back to the computer screen.

"Also, please take these ridiculous flowers with you. I have enough desk clutter as is."

I scooped up my twelve-cut bouquet and set sail in confusion. This was beyond perplexing. I drifted back to my office and watched Louise from a distance. Within moments, she popped up from behind her station like a frightened gopher scurrying away to the nearest restroom. Something was off. I don't particularly know Louise, but all of the encounters with her have been pleasant until now. What changed, and why did the sudden attitude shift? Something was wrong. I didn't want to think about it or even say it, for that matter. But my gut never lies. This was the Night Script. I hate to say it but I think Alvin should be looped in on this.

Drip, drop, drip, drop tapped the leaky sink.

"Stupid, stupid, stupid! Why did I lash out like that? Phoebe probably thinks I'm crazy now. What the heck had come over me?"

Louise knew this wasn't her. She may have been a klutz and a little anxious at times, but she was never aggressive. Hunching over the sink, she began to splash the cool waters of New York tap upon her brow.

"Ugh, I feel so clammy. Am I getting sick? Great, absolutely the last thing I need," whispered Louise.

Louise could tell she was off, but that's no excuse. She felt as if she owed Phoebe an apology. Perhaps seeing Phoebe so happy in her moment with that Darius guy made her a tad jealous, she thought. Her mind raced, pounding with agony as a migraine seemed to be setting in.

"I gotta get it together. Come on, Lou, just go out there, put your game face on, and smooth things out."

But before she could touch the polished door handle, a raspy voice danced up the hairs of her neck.

"You owe that stranger nothing." It hissed.

Louise quickly turned her head, brushing a series of bouncy curls from her eye.

"Is this a joke? Okay, not funny."

Slowly pacing the restroom, she peeked under each stall. Awkward, sure, but a series of feet would be far less unsettling. But in true horror fashion, no one was there.

"Don't fret, child. It's simply you and I."

"Whoever is saying that I'm getting security! This isn't funny!"

Louise made haste to the door but couldn't help but notice a large figure looming behind her within the mirror's reflection. A tall, muscular creature with the body of a man, but his head was that of a fox. The creature stretched its arms, revealing a large set of bat wings. Before she could scream, her body fell limp, and she began to hover feet above the restroom counter. The once bright florescent lighting flickered like that of an old subway car as Louise's eyes rolled back into her skull. Truly drowning in fear as she grasped her throat for air, only to produce a faint yelp.

"Make no mistake, sweet youth. For this isn't death, but the gift of life. Now utter the words."

"No. Please, no!" cried Louise.

"Say it. Thou knows what must be said."

"Tu et ego…" she whispered.

Falling flat to the floor, she began to come to it. Was this a dream? Was I dead? Everything seemed enhanced. The once dim lights were now as bright as diamonds flickering within the sun. Louise examined her palm. Steam was radiating from the flexion creases, and not to mention, her caramel-colored skin was now glowing to a hum. Small bits of electricity were weaving within her veins, but that was not all that had seemed to change. She felt confident and more sure of herself than ever before. Pulling herself to her feet, steadying her balance like that of a baby deer, Louise looked deep into the mirror. The creature was there again, looming over her shoulder like a proud father, resting his Goliath hand upon her collarbone.

"How do you feel, child? Is this new power not invigorating?"

Louise had to admit she felt little to no shame. This feeling was indeed amazing. She had never felt power and assurance of this kind. She was no longer afraid. If anything, she had succumbed to the creature's seduction.

"Who…what are you? Why me? This feeling is…"

"Bliss, is it not? I suppose a brief history lesson is in order. I am a creature, not bound to this fiergen. I have spent all of an ecnes simply searching for my freedom. I am the delegate of the Trionfi. I am the Naberius of the Seraphim bound to Solomon. I am Gamigin."

"Are you some sort of ghost or monster?" inquired Louise, seemingly now fearless of the creature before her.

"Ghost, ha!" chuckled Gamigin.

"No, I am simply a being on a mission to free his Section from imprisonment beyond the net. And you, my dear Louise, are going to help me. With your allegiance to me, all of thou desires will come to fruition, for I am you, and you are I."

Louise gazed deeply into the mirror, noticing that her glasses were no longer needed as her vision had become perfect. Not to mention, the beauty being reflected superseded previous bashfulness. For the first time in her life, she felt beautiful, confident, and powerful. How could she possibly resist the stranger's offer?

"Wow, this is crazy! Suppose I take you up on your offer. What else is possible?"

"Hum, possibilities are nothing but limits set by the mind. With me at the helm, nothing is out of our reach," purred Gamigin.

"Open your right hand and repeat after me."

"Ignis enchant."

Louise tightly closed her eyes, doing exactly as Gamigin asked, stretching out her right hand as far as possible and opening her palm to the ceiling. It was strange, but she began to feel oddly comfortable with the creature, for this was the first time in her life she felt appreciated and accepted.

"Concentrate, my dear. Let me guide you."

Whoosh! With her eyes to a clamp, Louise turned her face as she could feel the warmth of something brilliant. She had done it, opening but one eye; she was now face to face with the manifestation of a ball of fire in the palm of her hand. Louise was in shock. She moved left, then right, then up and down, astonished at how the ball of fire stayed with her.

"Look at that," smiled Gamigin. *"A great flame bright and beautiful, but merely an ember amongst your grace."*

Louise was head over heels, quickly agreeing with Gamigin's demand.

"Teach me, can you teach me more? This is incredible!"

"I know what it is that you seek, Louise, for I am you."

"And you are I," she replied.

"Good, now let us find it." Smiled Gamigin.

"Find what?" asked Louise. Clueless to the events unraveling before her very eyes.

Gamigin puffed up, bulking in size, his amber-colored pupils now burning a hot red in a sea of black sclera.

"The most powerful book in existence, my prison, and salvation: 'The Night Script'"

Chapter Seven
Angle shades

A s I paced wall to wall in my office, my once-good mood had completely soured. I was worried about Louise. I truly didn't understand what had gone wrong. I plopped down into my chair, hoping to piece the puzzle together, replaying the entire interaction frame by frame in my mind. Then I noticed it, the Night Script, but something was off about its placement. I'm 100 percent positive I left it closed on my desk, yet here it is wide open. No way someone could have come in here. I always lock my door behind me when I leave, even if it's just for a second. Scanning the book's texts with my fingertips, I could feel the warmth radiating from its pages. Some of the words even sparkled a bit. Something was up, but never mind that for now, it looks as if Louise is finally out of the restroom. Maybe she just had to blow off a little steam. I've been there a time or two in my life. I'll check back with her tomorrow morning. But it's about that time to punch the clock, and against my personal feelings, I think I need to speak with Alvin.

Something about this all felt urgent. The minute my feet touched the pavement, I spit out that oh-so-famous incantation.

"Tu et ego. Alvin, Alvin, we need to talk. Now!"

"Hey Phoebe, I was thinking the same thing. Look, I know…"

"Save it. Look, I think something is going on with the Night Script Al."

I could feel the tension in Alvin's body. He was just as nervous as I was. *"What do you mean, Pheebs? Did something happen while I was sleeping?"*

"No, I mean Yes, well maybe. Long story short, Darius came to visit me today, and I asked Louise out for girls' night, and she became, well, I don't know, angry, I guess. And I couldn't shake the feeling that something was in the air. It felt as if a presence was in the office. Then, the Night Script moved, I think, but I'm not 100 percent sure. I don't know, Al, something just feels off!"

My mind was starting to outpace my mouth, flipping and fumbling one thought after another.

"Okay, okay, relax and just breathe. When you say something was in the air, what did it feel like?"

"Ugh god, I'm not sure, Al. It felt eerie, just the entire interaction. Louise isn't like that, at least I don't think she is. And the Night Script, it was warm, like a pot that had been left to cool."

Alvin stopped dead in his tracks. I could feel his feet coming to an abrupt halt like a soldier during a march.

"Warm, wait, warm? Oh no, this isn't good. This isn't good at all, Phoebe."

"What, Alvin, what does this all mean? Tell me."

Alvin was brooding. I'd felt him upset before, but this was different. This was pure fear. He was afraid. I could feel the sweat beading upon his brow. His breathing became my breathing, frantic and wispy. He was frozen, a total deer in headlights, but now is not the time. I need answers and fast.

"Alvin, what is going on?" A loaded question that I felt I knew the answer to.

"Alvin, snap out of it!"

"It means he's free, Phoebe. He's out of the book. And If I was a betting man, I'd say your friend Louise is in a lot of trouble. And the worst part of it all is, she probably doesn't even realize it."

Alvin and I quickly made our way back to my apartment. If anything, we need to confirm our theory of Gamigin possessing Louise before taking action, but how? Alvin assured me the signs of possession would be obviously unobvious, whatever that means. I have to admit a side of me was feeling that rush again, the child-like intrigue I felt upon first hearing Alvin's stories.

"Buzz, buzz, buzz."

I looked down at my phone vibrating dangerously close to the edge of the table. It was Darius, ugh my heart wanted to answer, I really, really do. But he shouldn't be mixed up in this mess any more than he already is.

"Are you going to answer that?" chimed Alvin. I could feel his cheeky grin slowly emerging.

"Hey, look, I'm not mad or anything. He's a good-looking guy, and it's obvious you really like him. My only advice is to be as honest as possible with him, even with the weird stuff."

Alvin had a point. I could tell he had done a bit of self-reflecting over the past day or so. It was starting to feel like we were in sync again.

"Phoebe, I know you don't want to hear it, but I am sorry. I was being selfish. I hope we can get past this."

He was sincere, and this time, my body could feel he truly meant his apology. He was warming up. His goosebumps and butterflies were now mine. It even felt as if he were crying a bit.

"I'm sorry, Alvin. I could have reacted better. It's just, ya know, with everything I've been through in the past month or so has just been, I have just been…I don't know, on edge."

"It's a lot, I get it. But you're doing great, Pheebs. I'm going to fix all of this, I promise. Now, let's figure out what's going on with this Night Script and your friend. And ya know what, call Darius over. Heck, I'm sure he knows plenty already. Take it from a pro: leaving a loved one in the dark isn't the best strategy."

Embracing Alvin's advice, I reached out to Darius. It was now 10 pm, and the clock was ticking. Alvin, Darius, and I now sat in my apartment dissecting the strange events of the day. Alvin even cooked up a spell that would allow Darius to hear him speak. It was interesting, the two unknown rivals now chatting it up like a couple of teenage boys. Who would have thought?

"So, here's what I think we should be on the lookout for. According to my mother's journal, Gamigin changed my Aunt Caroline's entire attitude. If Louise is under his control, maybe we'll see a similar outcome. Not to mention, if he's using possession, he's not strong enough to take a physical form, I'm guessing."

"Good point, Al, but do you think he'll attack as well? This is New York City, not some tiny village. A lot of people could be in danger."

"Look, obviously, you two know a bit more about this stuff than me." Butted *Darius*

"But I think it's best to do this all from a distance. It sounds like this thing can be a little volatile if you ask me."

"Darius is right." Wow, Alvin swallowing his ego is a new one.

"Careful is the word of the day. We have to respect Gamigin's power as well as the fact that Louise is just a puppet in all of this, just as my aunt was."

The stakes seemed to be getting higher and higher, but no way was I going to let this creature just wreak havoc. Not in my city! My confidence has grown a lot, and I knew as much as Alvin and Darius wanted to help, it was up to me.

"Look, you two, as much as I want this to be a team effort. I'm the one in the office with Louise, not to mention I have access to her calendar and schedule. Let's face it: once I cross those doors into Monarch, it's a one-woman mission."

I could feel Alvin and Darius' emotions running high. They wanted to do everything in their power to help, but the duo was well aware of the truth. This was my friend, my office, my intel, and my show.

Tonight was an odd night. Darius ended up staying over, as it was far too late for him to return home. I was nervous at first, but Darius had a knack for melting my woes away. It was comforting; nothing happened, but something about being in his arms all night felt right, soothing, and stress-free. Neither of us spoke, but it was perfect. It was as if we were riding the wave of each other's thoughts, pure respite. The two of us would soon wake up to the rhythm of NY morning rain against my window; nights never seem to last long enough, and today was a big day. I was nervous and had no idea what I was getting into. Darius assured me that everything would be as smooth as glass. Easy for Mr. Cool to say sure.

"Hey, relax, Pheebs. Just remember it will be obviously unobvious." Coached Alvin via train ride in.

I sent Alvin away as I approached Monarch's lobby. Usually, I would go to my office and make it a point to zone out, just me in my own little world. Today, of course, was a bit different. I decided to set up camp in the break room, as it had the best vantage point to the elevators. Noisy, noisy, noisy! Clanging coffee mugs, groggy morning yawns, water cooler banter, and a feeding frenzy for the best Keurig cups. I had to keep a low profile, taking more time than I normally would curating my coffee and awkwardly making small talk with Monarch employees I had never even seen before. This tactic consisted mostly of a lot of smiling and head nodding on my end, slowly shifting my vision to the elevators waiting for her arrival.

The clock read 9:05. Either she's a bit late, or something is up. But low and behold, just as I began to raise my Anthora cup to my lips, those infamous elevator doors skimmed open, and Louise came strutting out. I had to blink twice, lifting my glasses and swiping the sand from my weary eyes. It was definitely her, but my goodness, talk about obviously unobvious. She was jaw-dropping! So much for never getting a single flower; I have a feeling that's about to change.

Every guy in the office looked like that yellow drool emoji. Her hair was straight, pulled back into a masterfully braided ponytail. Gone were the bouncy curls, replaced with an unnatural deep black. Everything about her had more edge. She was stunning, from her burgundy-colored lipstick to her sleek black form-fitting dress, fire-red nails, and Oxford pumps. God, she's in shape. She's built like a tennis player with the strut of a runway model. Even her black fur coat draped over her tattooed arm screamed fashionista. Either this was one heck of a makeover, or the Devil possessing her has amazing taste. I could only help but wonder which one of these Monarch pigs was going to shoot his shot first. Ding, ding, ding! Looks like we have a winner, a slick-back gray suit guy. Look at him scuttling over like a bottom-feeder crab.

"Hem, hem. Hello gorgeous, are you new here? If so, I'd be more than happy to show you around." Asked the overconfident employee.

Interestingly enough, Louise just stood there with a blank stare on her face. Her eyes were cold but ever so hypnotic, casting a spell with every bat of her bewitching long lashes. The slow chewing and popping of her gum only reinforced her disinterest. This guy was out of his league. This version of Louise was built differently.

"Silent type, huh? Actually, let me just cut to it. How about you and I go out for some drinks after work? New York can be a bit rough, but don't worry, beautiful, I do CrossFit. I'll protect you."

The gray suit man reached out his hand in an effort to touch Louise, but before it could register, Louise snatched the jerk's hand out of thin air. Based on his yelp, she must have grabbed a pressure point or something. It's as if she had studied Kung Fu for years.

"In case you've forgotten," said Louise in a low but stern tone, twisting his wrist and sending him into a series of painful grimaces.

"Unwanted touch is a form of harassment. My recommendation: don't. Or next time, it will be more than your wrist that gets twisted."

Louise released the suit, leaving him clutching his wrist in agony. Sure, he was physically hurt, but I'd wager it was his ego that truly took the hit. All of this was entertaining, to say the least, but not enough to confirm possession. I need more proof. Throughout the day, I did my best to keep a close eye on Louise. Her daily actions seemed normal enough, I suppose. She was dialed into her office duties, ignoring the surrounding banter as if it were white noise. Maybe we really do have this all wrong, or so I thought. It was getting close to quitting time, so I made arrangements to meet Darius after work to bring him up to speed. As I began gathering my items, I spotted Louise walking towards my office.

Tap, tap, tap.

She was outside of my door, her sharp red index nail pitter-pattering against the glass.

"Oh hey, Louise, come on in. How has your day been?"

She gave me the classic 'I won't hurt you, white woman grin' before moving on with her inquiry.

"I spoke with Garrett today, and he wanted me to…."

It's happening again, Louise paused mid-sentence. Oh no. I won't fall for that one again. I'll let her have her moment. Her eyes were blank. She was fixated on my bag for some reason, and maybe I'm going crazy, but I don't recall Louise having silver eyes.

"That's an interesting-looking book," said Louise with an unsure smirk as she glanced at the Night Script.

111

"It's a very unique-looking book. May I take a look at it?"

My throat dried up as if I had drunk a glass of gravel. Crap, I had forgotten the stupid book was in my bag, this isn't good! I had to think fast, so I blurted out the first lie that came to my mind.

"Actually, it's kind of in the middle of a restoration process. Ya know, it's just really fragile. White glove treatment kinda thing."

"Of course, I totally understand. Anyway, Garrett asked me to give these documents to you. Have fun."

I could practically taste the sarcasm in the air as she slammed the manila folder on my desk. I'm more certain than ever that Gamigin is in control of Louise. The odd behavior was one thing, but the interest in the Night Script seems a bit obvious. I have to inform the others ASAP.

I dashed out of the office at speeds that I didn't know I was even capable of.

"Huff, Huff, Tu et huff, huff, ego.

"Yawn. Oh hey, Pheebs, how did the recon go?"

At first, I stood blank unsure of how to even answer Alvin's question. But too much was on the line for me to sugarcoat data. Louise was under a spell. I had seen enough, and it was our duty to save her. I took a deep breath and gave Alvin all of my findings.

"Silver eyes, increased confidence with a splash of aggression, topped off with a sudden interest in the Night Script. Yeah, it sounds legit to me. We don't have much time. I'm sure Gamigin could sense the Night Script. He made the mistake of losing and underestimating its power once. Doubtful he'll do it twice. We need a plan."

It was time to break out the old whiteboard. Later that night, Alvin, Darius, and I scribbled ideas and strategies to potentially extract Gamigin, but this was all in vain. The spell previously used to trap him was long gone. It was a dead end. But one thing was certain: The Night Script had to go back into hiding, so we couldn't run the risk of Gamigin and Louise stealing it. Without hesitation, the mystical text was placed back in the cloak of darkness between the counters. Funny something so powerful is residing now with the insignificant crumbs of yesteryear, but it's for the best. Later that night, it was more of the same sense of uncertainty. God, I'm dreading tomorrow. I couldn't shake the feeling of trouble in my future. There was no way I was going to be able to avoid Louise all day, and she was beyond unpredictable. Now that she knows that I have the Night Script, she's going to make my life a living hell.

Sleeping was out of the question. All night long, I lay awake thinking of all of the ways Louise was going to torture me. What she did to the gray suit man was nothing. Ugh, how are we ever going to fix this mess? After a knackering night of tossing and turning, with brief dreams of Louise biting my head off, it was back to Monarch. The entire morning, I sat in my office on edge. Every knock, bump, or ding sent me into a jumping tizzy. I needed to get a hold of myself, and with that ray of pep talk, my logic began to kick in. Ha, Louise wouldn't risk killing me! Gamigin would never know where the Night Script is, right? I'm safe, safe for sure. It's too bad my self-reassurance went right down the drain as soon as Louise waltzed in. Man, you've got to be kidding me! She's even more regal-looking than she was yesterday. No one should be allowed to be evil and look this good. We made eye contact from across the hall, the feeling of fear pumping through my veins.

Talk about if looks could kill. Her ice-cold silver eyes jabbed my heart like two daggers, and as if that wasn't tortuous enough, her carmine lips brandished a confident smirk. This was a mental fight she was playing at, and so far, she had me in a chokehold. I can't do this. I needed some air, water, or something. Springing to my feet, I made a move to the office kitchen.

"Hey, Kiddo."

"Ahhhhhhh," I screeched, spilling the cool ice water down my sleeve!

"Oh my God, Garrett, it's just you. I'm so sorry."

"Whoa. Didn't mean to spook you, kid. Umm, is everything alright?"

Oh, Garrett, how I wish I could tell you the truth, but I couldn't possibly drag another person into this nonsense.

"Umm, yeah, everything is just great."

"Good, glad to hear," smiled Garrett.

Garrett began to look around as if he were some sort of spy, adjusting his glass, followed by a stroke of his frosty speckled hair.

"Psst," he gestured, raising his index signaling me to lean in close.

"Hey, so I heard back from the Publishing house in London. I think I have the green light, Kiddo," whispered Garrett.

"What? No way! This is so exciting, congrats!" I *said,* clapping my hands over my mouth to hide my secretive smile.

"Congrats to you too, kid, we're going to the top!" smiled Garrett as I gave him the biggest of hugs.

"This is so exciting." I was trying my hardest not to show my glee, but this was a huge moment not just for Garrett's career but mine as well.

"We need to celebrate, and it's a must this time. No backing out, Garrett!"

"Absolutely Pheebs. Gosh, Sarah would have loved London."

Garrett's face went stern. I could see the pain in his eyes. I had completely forgotten about Sarah; she was so young, not that much older than I was. This must be hard for him, so much change in such a short time. Garrett doesn't mention her much, but no doubt he's still dealing with grief. I gave Garrett one last hug and congrats before heading back towards my office. I hate seeing him so sad.

Walking back to my office, my mind was in Lala Land. I couldn't believe what was happening. This could be my big break! Whatever dread poisoning the office air slowly drifted away as I began to daydream of my first published novel. Ahh, what a life. No more tell-alls, gossip, or steamy love guru nonsense. Just fiction, beautiful fiction, fresh from the banks of my imagination. And to top it off, London, the gardens, the architecture, and a proper cup of tea. But within my excitement, I noticed a small hiccup, Louise. She was leaning against the wall outside of the break room. Had she been there the entire time just watching? She uncrossed her arms, leaned forward, and slowly strutted away with a grin. Her clicking heels echoed down the hall as she disappeared into the nook of her desk. Uh-oh, this isn't good. I feel like she's up to something. The question is, what?

Chapter Eight

Scarce Blue Tigers

Within the gloomy halls of a prewar Queensborough apartment, a series of black candles melted within the wells of their chambersticks. The once bright double-pane windows that often provided a gateway to daydreams in between light sips of coffee were now covered in scribbles of magic circles and sigils. Manuscript after Manuscript, journal after journal, lay discarded across the floor like parade confetti. A series of unnatural plant vines now invaded the chipped wooden crown molding, adding to the already poor visibility. But even stranger elements danced within the milieu as a dense purple mist drifted throughout the premise. Louise seemed unfazed with her eyes now dark from the thick, runny liner, she fixated on a makeshift fox shrine a few paces away. Louise's silver eyes now rolled to the back of her skull as her hands began to carve symbols into the blonde wood floors.

"The Night Athame, Midworld Pendulum. The great feed of Prana, life to Gamigin." Louie's motions seemed erratic yet beautiful, like a dance off-key. But it was evident her body was not her own.

"Master Gamigin, I believe a discovery has been made," she whispered.

With all of her might, Louise Plunged a dagger into the floor, the hilt of the knife swaying back and forth. As the blade's movements came to a halt, a disembodied voice rang throughout the cluttered flat. The booming voice echoed and bounced from wall to wall, forcing the metal radiator pipes to vibrate.

"Speak, child!" yawned the voice.

"The Night Scripts whereabouts, Master. It would seem that good fortune has smiled upon us. I have reason to believe an individual within the walls of Monarch possesses it. I could feel its energy. There's no mistaking it."

"Your instincts serve you well, as I have felt it too."

A large glass pyramid filled with light appeared before Louise, snapping her out of her trance with its luminosity. Inside the structure was grainy footage of Phoebe embracing Garrett within the break room, as well as her having conversations with Alvin and Darius.

"It would seem this Miss Graham holds many secrets close to her heart."

"Close to her heart? You mean the boyfriend, master?"

"Close, my dear, very close," chuckled Gamigin.

"Our bond is becoming more in sync. As the days pass, we are even beginning to think as one. Poor little Phoebe Graham is indeed obsessed with a man. Yet, not one of vanity, but one stricken by grief. A symbol of comfort, a barbarous reminder of the father figure she never had. Alas, this man is in pain, wearing various types of masks to conceal his misery.

"Our tactic is simple: his sorrow will be my hostage. She will either relinquish my Night Script or watch him succumb to grief under my gaze.

"What if she refuses, Master?"

"Then I will drain the woes from his soul and feast on his life force. And even when she surrenders, Mr. Miller will be feasted upon. He will be more than enough fuel for me to take a physical form."

"Brilliant as always, master, but if I may inquire, why is this text so important? You are so close to life. Once you feed upon Mr. Garrett, you will be an absolute power, and with no spell available to seal you within its pages again, what purpose doesn't serve?"

A shadowy finger seemed to reach out from the void, raising Louise's chin with its trenchant claw.

"You truly are blooming, Louise, as is your lust for knowledge and power. Its only rivalry would be your effulgent beauty. The Night Script will only aid in your growth, tis a powerful tool full of spells and incantations as old as the cosmos. Belphegor is a crafty one. He uses powerful magic to conceal his location. Yet, there is one known spell capable of seeing past his trickery. That spell being Sempiternal Eye, which I will use to locate the traitor and commandeer the device in his possession. Once free, my brothers and I will rule the human world as kings and you, my darling, as my queen."

A small tear bubbled and rolled down Louise's cheek. No one had ever shared such kind words with her. Gamigin may not be a human nor a lover, but his compassion was undeniable to her. In her mind, he was the romantic she had always dreamed of.

"Belphegor is a fugitive from the Eidolon Plateau, in possession of the only known tool capable of opening Ogun's net. The only barrier standing between my brethren and our conquest of the bounty of souls here on

119

earth. The wisdom I am going to bestow upon you is eons old. Very few humans have heard this tale, not even your predecessor, yet you are different, Louise. I am comfortable with you, and I trust your investment in our nexus."

With a wave of his ghastly claw, the glowing pyramid displayed a new image within its tenebrous mist. A world long gone, fragments from a plain beyond our own. Kaleidoscope pieces stitched together in proper order, revealing a recalcitrant past.

"Blood was just the beginning. A loss today does not define our future...

After the Hierophant War came the surrender of the Trionfi Knights, a Section of 15 Devils were locked in an eternal rivalry with God's most trusted angels. After centuries of battles, only 12 of the Trionfi remained. Disappointed and depleted, the remaining Trionfi were forced to kneel before the victorious hand of God and his angels, swearing off the assault of humankind. With no options in hand, unanimity was given to preserve our survival. Devils were limited to feeding on only the cruelest souls of humans. No more, no less. A cruel fate, as this bounty would be small, no more than scraps to feed many.

But one must never underestimate the intelligence of humankind. If one is not cruel, one cannot be eaten, a simple yet effective assessment. Our legion was a mockery, Devils, ha! First bested by Angels, now bested by mere humans. Devils are creatures that have little emotion, yet mortification would seem to be the only relatable feeling within our ranks. As the ages passed, our recalcitrance grew, the hand of God became trivial, and gone were the bylaws as the time for diplomacy had expired.

One by one, our Section overindulged in the feasting of human souls. The wicked, the righteous, the wealthy, the poor, none were granted amnesty as our appetites raged. Displeased with our infraction, God commanded the angels to bring justice to this coup. The Angels, selfish in their own right, took joy in slaying two more of my remaining brethren, an opportunity they had long been salivating for. Death was simply too noble in God's eyes. No, his punishment would be far more vicious: banishment to the Eidolon Plateau.

Eidolon rested within the fabric of time itself, no night, no day, just a void, an endless void surrounded by rocky terrain and brimstone. One could go mad simply by walking in a circle. Yet, in true fashion, banishment was not enough. In order to prevent even the slightest chance of a breach, God created the Ogun Net, the great contingency plan. Should we ever make it beyond the void, the net's power would keep us sealed. The madness, ten devils, deprived, insane, starving, it's a miracle we didn't kill one another. Life in this hell was taking its toll; all seemed hopeless, or so we thought. While the nine of us wallowed in sorrow, Belphegor, the most cunning of our pack and an alchemist beyond his years, created a tool capable of forcing a rip through any sort of protective magic, including the net, the *Volkman's Stone.* Just one flaw: the stone required souls to power it. In its current state, the stone only had enough power for only one of us to pass through. Seeing as Belphegor was the most familiar with the functionality of the stone, it was decided he would go.

Hours turned to days, days shifted to what felt like months as we waited for his return. Perhaps the Angels destroyed him? Belphegor was cunning but far from a great warrior. Was brother another loss in the conquest for freedom? Then, a strange message appeared. An anonymous scroll guided by feathers sent from the heavens, slipping oh so easily through the net. Belphegor had betrayed us! He accepted a deal from God himself, agreeing never to use the stone. In return, he would be granted sole ownership of the wicked souls in the human realm. It was one thing to lose to the Angels, but never in a trillion years of purgatory did we think one of our own would betray us.

Defeated yet again, my brothers and I were left licking our wounds. Perhaps this was destiny, or…perhaps not. Three days after Belphegor's betrayal, stricken by failure, I wondered about the void. I had never ventured this far from our encampment. The heat was blaring, and gasping for air seemed useless. Delirious and confused, I began to dig. Clawing and scraping the stale soil, blood leaking from the tips of my claws, not sure of what I was looking for. That's when I stumbled across the Night Script. Eons and eons of script, written in some of the oldest languages that I had ever seen. Mystified and rejuvenated by my discovery, I raced back to camp, presenting my find to my brothers. Ninja, the elder of our group, recognized the ancient book almost immediately.

He informed us that it possessed the powers of our forefathers, a book designed and crafted by Devils more malevolent than we could ever imagine. Only the immensely powerful could wield or speak its eloquences without succumbing to its life-draining properties. The elder preached that the book is a lost cause and that none of us possess the strength to use its magic, hence why it was banished to Eidolon, too. But in my eyes, that was a fallacy. The book called to me why I did not know. The well of knowledge has been kind to me in my lifetime. I am wise enough to know some things happen for a reason and ambitious enough not to let an opportunity slip through my fingers.

For what felt like centuries, I studied and practiced the incantations within the text, perfecting my abilities and pushing my limits to the brink of death itself. With my sorcery knowledge now at its acme, I presented my power to my brethren by ripping a hole in the Ogun Net with only time and size for one of us to pass through.

Ninja was wrong. I may not rival the power of the Devils of old, but I had been chosen. As I Passed through the net, I could see the rift closing beneath my feet. Where was I? It was as if I had been spat into the cosmos. Beautiful orbs floated in front of me, each showing a different blip in time. I had no control over the direction in which the orbs pulled. Helpless, I was tossed into one of the spheroids, the space around me now reflecting a snowy terrain. It would be days before I came to it. The stress of the book's power now taking an even greater toll on my body than originally anticipated. If Ninja saw me in this pitiful state, he would surely rub my nose in it. Perhaps he was correct in his assessment after all. My eyes darted from side to side, gathering information on my would-be whereabouts. I made an effort to rise to my feet, but I was weak, dying even. The thought of hope began to drift away like steam from hot brimstone. That's when I saw her, your predecessor Caroline.

Gamigin went silent. The room began to feel hollow and small, his booming voice missing from the surroundings. Was it possible that a creature of his kind actually loved a human?

Louise brushed the wispy dark hairs from her eyes, *"What happened to her, my Lord? Do go on."*

"She...she was taken from me, and I was forced to remain confined to the pages of the Night Script. I was so close, close to being back to my normal self, close to freeing my brothers, and that ungrateful witch took it away from me. She took her away from me!"

The room began to shake vigorously. A small vase in the corner bounced about like a child's pogo stick until crashing to the floor.

"But make no mistake, my dear, this foible will not be exploited again. This time, I will not be denied!"

"Understood, Master. So, what is our next move? What action do you wish me to take?"

"This hurdle, this Phoebe, we must take caution as we know not what sorcery she may possess. I feel she may be receiving guidance from an unworldly source. Caution is key, as I am near completion and refuse to be returned to that dreaded tomb of a book."

The ghostly image of Gamigin appeared before Louise, reaching out his hand and picking up a piece of the shattered vase only to have it pass through his hand in a matter of seconds.

"One more large feed should be adequate. That man in your office, Garrett Miller, has suffered great loss in his lifetime. I can feel it. He is a shell of his former self; all that keeps him going is his own guilt and father-like drive for Phoebe. His sorrow will not only be my restoration, but the bargaining chip for my Night Script.

Louise, my dear, tomorrow, visit this Garrett Miller, get him away from curious eyes. I shall handle the rest."

"Bzzzt bzzzt bzzzt."

Ugh, these mornings never get any easier! I sat up, rubbing my grainy eyes, only to view a few good morning messages from Darius. But my mind just wasn't there yet. All I kept seeing was that image of Louise crossing her arms, seeming so sure of herself. That was a sign, a warning shot pointed directly at me, I'm sure. If I were a betting girl, I'd say she and her Devil buddy found a way to get the Night Script off of me. I'm going to have to stay on my toes, one step ahead even. Ahh, who am I kidding? How the heck am I supposed to stay one step ahead if I can't even see what's coming? Glancing at the microwave clock, it was clear my brooding would have to wait. I'm running behind, as is, and today is the big day, Trembly's big book reveal. Thank God for calendar reminders. The last thing I need are monsters like the Terror Twins breathing down my neck, and they are far more relentless than witchcraft and Devils.

Dashing to my stop, I was able to swing my arm through the closing door without a fraction of time to spare. Of course, in classic New York fashion, today's extra special day kicked off with an extra special train packed to the gills with all walks of New York's highest and…New York's lowest, beautiful. As I slowly wiggled my way between a man carrying a massive cello, a lady with five suitcases, and, oddly enough, a guy holding a snake, it didn't seem as if I was off to a glowing start. Thankfully, the train car cleared a bit at the following stop, allowing for an open seat. As I plopped down into a seat, one of my earbuds bounced to the disgusting car floor.

"Fantastic."

Gingerly leaning over to retrieve the rouge headphone, I was greeted by a very perturbing voice. A voice that I wasn't fully prepared to deal with.

"Oh, my, fancy meeting you here!"

My stomach flipped inside out. It couldn't be, but it certainly was…Louise. I was alone and cornered, my eyes focusing on the sharpness of her leather thigh-high boots and lengthy pea coat. Lifting my head slowly in trepidation, I could feel my lips beginning to quiver as words leaked out of my mouth, keeping my equanimity seemed to be flying out the window.

"Oh hey, Louise!" I stupidly laughed.

My hands were shaking like an old church ladies' tambourine. I could barely get my headphones back in their case.

"What are the odds of meeting you here? That's so funny."

Funny, yeah funny, good one, Pheebs, there's nothing remotely funny about this. Try terrifying.

"How about that big reveal today, eh? I saw it on Garrett's calendar. I'm sure he's just thrilled," joked Louise, tapping her red claw-like nails on the tip of her lip.

God, making eye contact with her was like looking at a solar eclipse. She has to know that I'm petrified by now, but I have to stand firm.

"I think we have a best seller on our hands again. I mean, Garrett never misses a beat, and the Terror Twins sure know how to market a product."

"Haha, is that your name for them, The Terror Twins? I actually find them to be quite a treat."

With a big gulp of swallowed spit, I managed to force a gentle laugh in agreement. Time was at a standstill. Finally, between our conversation, we reached yet another stop. The remaining train riders scurried to the platform, leaving me and Louise to ride the remainder of our commute in awkwardness. I tried to seem as normal as possible, but those big gray eyes just kept staring at me, analyzing me from head to toe, particularly glancing at the courier bag on my hip. I see what was going on here. She was looking for the Night Script.

"Ding. Stand clear of the closing doors, please!"

Yes! Saved by the subway guy.

"Welp gotta go, Louise, I'll see you in the office. I just want to grab a quick bite before the hustle starts. Well, hey, happy hunting. I mean, good day or, um, see you later."

I could still feel Louise's eyes in the distance. I dashed up the flight of steps like a deer fleeing a hunter. I didn't think I could move that fast. My heart was racing as I popped into a nearby coffee shop. I had to tell Alvin about this.

"Tu et ego."

"Oh hey, Pheebs, I thought you'd be in the office by now. It's odd that you're not. Everything okay?"

"No, Alvin, everything is not 'okay.'" I hurled, gesturing air quotes sarcastically.

"It's Louise. She was on the train with me this morning. I dropped one of my headphones, and bam, she was right in front of me. What are the odds she

would be riding the exact same train as me at the exact same time!"

"Pretty high, actually. I mean, the city of New York houses about eight million people, and tons of them ride different trains...."

"That's not the point, Alvin! The point is it was creepy, and she's definitely up to something."

I could feel Alvin pacing back and forth inside of my head. He was trying to formulate a reason as well as a plan, but he was stuck, just like me. There was only one thing that we could do: wait. Just pull up our bootstraps, sit on the sidelines, and wait.

As I exited the coffee shop, I peered over my shoulder over and over again, but Louise was long gone. For the most part, it appeared as if the morning would be rather quiet, but I've been in this position before, and knowing the Twins and their affinity for eleven-o-clock meetings, total chaos was about to break loose.

"Knock, knock, knock." It was Garrett at my office door. It was time to hear our fate.

Garrett and I made haste to the elevator.

"Well, kiddo, this is it. I looked over your notes, and let me just be the first to say you're truly coming into your own. I think the Twins and Trembly are going to love it. Or at least let's hope so."

Yeah, let's hope so, but that was the least of my worries at the moment. With the numbers above us slowly ticking to our destination, I was met with a very unwanted surprise. As the janky doors skid opened, we were greeted by none other than Louise.

"Oh, hello there! Garrett, you look dashing as ever today. Ready for the meeting?"

"Ready as I'm gonna be." He smiled.

I couldn't help but look in her direction. Man, it should be illegal to look that good AND be that delightful. Leaning into the elevator's silver guardrail, Louise scanned me again like a tiger waiting to make its kill.

"Is everything alright, Phoebe? You seem a bit off-color."

She's toying with me again.

"Yeah, just ya know the jitters, this stuff always gets to me."

That's it! I was officially fed up with this. I refused to let this woman just think she could bully me. As we walked into the blazingly lit boardroom, tension hung thick in the air like a storm cloud on the verge of unleashing its fury. The tell-all meeting had entered discussion, but unbeknownst to the colorful cast of elites with conflicting opinions, it was that of the two least influential figures in the room on opposite sides of the battlefield. Louise and I locked eyes, this time my gaze unwavering. It was as if the boardroom had become an arena, and we were the gladiators competing for a coveted prize of ego and wits. Sweat began to bead on my forehead, but there was no way I was backing down. I was dialed in. I couldn't even hear Trembly's gloating.

"I think we have another hit on our hands, Amber Lynn. You've done it again!" swooned Trembly. I definitely heard that comment. He's gotta be kidding. The only thing Amber Lynn or Payton ever did for this novel was provide a poorly catered lunch with limited portions. But my fuming would have to settle for the back burner as Chris was preparing to interrupt.

"Team, team, excellent job with this piece. We have another hit on our hands thanks to the brilliant mind of Monsieur Sean V. Trembly!"

The meeting room broke into a thunderous applause.

Look at this nitwit Trembly, cupping both hands together, shaking them over his shoulders like he's winning an Oscar. Just the sight of him makes my stomach do back flips.

"Team, team, thank you for all of your efforts. How about we celebrate this momentous occasion with a bit of drink!" shouted Trembly.

My very soul was annoyed and irritated, but I couldn't take my eye off the ball. Louise seemed to be inching her way in my direction, but she shifted. Stopping mid-stride, she leaned over a leather chair to speak with Garrett. What is she playing at? Her conversation was with Garrett, though her eyes kept scowling in my direction. Louise's smile lit up the room as she gently touched Garrett's shoulder; they were laughing. Well, I give her credit. Her charm and charisma were undeniable. Garrett rose to his feet, exiting the room with Louise and the herd of employees, all heading towards the local bar for an evening of celebratory booze. Something is up. I had better tag along.

Ahh, McCarthy's Pub. Take it from a professional. If you are ever looking for a hive full of male toxicity, punching machines, gloating, and awful pickup lines, then this is the bar for you. As I brushed past each and every cookie-cutter jock that Monarch had to offer, I could see Louise and Garrett in the distance. Holding my glass paint at a 90-degree angle above my head, I slowly pushed through the crowd, trying my hardest to keep Louise in my sight.

"Phoebe, Phoebe Graham, was it?"

Wait, I was hallucinating? Amber Lynn, she's, umm, talking to me…

"Oh, hello, yes, that's me. Congratulations on another hit, Amber Lynn, brilliant."

Ugh, I can't believe those words even came out of my mouth.

"No, no need to congratulate me. It's you and the others that deserve the credit. I'm just the bankroll, sweetheart. But never mind that.

With a touch of sophistication, Amber Lynn proceeded to throw back a big gulp of her red wine.

"I just wanted to say stick with it. I'm hard, but only because I want you to succeed. Us women have to stick together, right?"

Wait, was I hearing this correctly? Where the heck am I? I would have never taken Amber Lynn as a feminist. Heck, I didn't even know she had a soul.

"Right, absolutely, I will do my best," I replied unconfidently.

"Just look at my idiot brother over there," gesturing a hitchhiker thumb over her shoulder towards Payton.

"I love him to pieces, but God, he's an idiot. If he can make strides, I'm sure you can make leaps. Keep pushing. Glass ceilings are for suckers."

Amber Lynn placed her finished glass back on the bar top, gave me a slight tap on the shoulder, and went back to brushing elbows with her fellow elites. Taking a gulp of my beer, filling my cheeks like a squirrel, I restarted my scan for Garrett and Louise. Oh no, they're gone. This isn't good!

131

"Tu et ego," I whispered.

"Alvin, I need your help. I can't find Garrett or Louise. I got caught up talking to Amber Lynn and lost sight of them."

"Damn, okay, Pheebs, let's ask around. Someone here must have seen them. How about the table next to the one they were sitting at?"

"Good call, Al."

Making my way through the crowd, I approached the table. Garrett's bag was present at the vacant table.

"Excuse me, Eddie, was it?" I pointed with a slight fog of memory.

I'm terrible with names, but I definitely remember seeing his name and photo in a Zoom meeting.

"Oh hey…. Phoebe, right?"

"Yup, that's me." I chuckled, followed by a stupid bow.

"I was going to ask if Garrett wanted another round. Have you, by chance, seen him?"

"Actually, he just stepped out with the new girl. Looked as if she had one too many already."

Without hesitation, I ran through the nearest door. They were long gone. Nothing but steam from striped pipes and a sea of people.

"Pheebs, this has a trap written all over it. No way they got away that fast. This is Gamigin's handy work, I'm sure of it."

"I can't just let them take him, Al!" I could feel the conviction spewing out of my voice box.

"Garrett is far more than just a boss to me. He's a mentor, no scratch that, a father. And I'll be damned if I let some monster have him!"

"And we won't let that happen, Pheebs. That much I can promise."

Alvin and I returned to the bar. It was time to regroup. We even pulled Darius into the loop. We need all the help we can get at this point.

As I went to retrieve Garrett's bag, a strange pink glow was emitting from underneath its worn leather. I'm guessing I was the only one who could see this, Alvin too.

"Al, are you seeing this?"

"Sure am, it's Draad magic. A thread leading us straight to the trap. We'd be wise not to follow until we have a plan. Let's get Darius and head back home."

Darius was waiting for me at the bottom of my apartment steps. I told him everything: the office stare down, Louise taking Garrett, and the strange pink trail. Darius was far too deep in this mess for shock. Making our way up the steps, we couldn't help but notice my apartment door was ajar.

"Wait," whispered Darius.

"Let me go in first."

And who said chivalry was dead, I thought sarcastically. However, Darius has a point: he's far larger than I. As we entered, a tall figure draped in black stood analyzing the various books scattered upon my shelf. It was beyond clear that this thing wasn't even close to being human. Its eyes emitted a silver glow through the eye slits of its mask.

"Who are you? You need to leave now!" boomed Darius.

"Leave?" chuckled the being.

"Oh, Ms. Graham, tis no way to treat a guest. Especially one willing to provide aid to your little problem."

The creature cleared his throat in a regalist fashion.

"Where are my manners? Please allow me to introduce myself...."

Chapter Nine

Orange Sulphur

When I was a little girl, my mother used to tell me, *"Sometimes it is best to just shut up and listen."*

I take it Darius was given different advice. Dashing across the room, charging the mysterious creature, he was stopped cold in his tracks…literally. Frozen by what appeared to be a beam of cold air, think car lights cutting through winter wind. As Darius' body came to a screeching halt, the color from his cheeks became barely visible, locking his mouth wide open like a taxidermy tiger's roar.

Running to his aide, I placed my hand on his cheek, quickly pulling back as it presented an icy sting.

"What have you done to him? Let him go now! If you've hurt a single hair on his head, I swear!"

"Relax, my lady, tis but minor Hygge *magic. Its' effects will wear off in a matter of minutes. Now, where was I? Ahh, yes, introductions were in order. Submit to the Nacht. It's thew a gift to my ichor we, the Trionfi Knights present to your undeserving eyes, Belphegor."*

Well, that was an introduction. The creature removed its draping black hood, his razor-sharp claws overlapping the tattered fabric. I couldn't believe my eyes. Alvin was experiencing the same, as I could feel his pupils expanding. Belphegor resembled a giant cat.

He was jet-black like that of a panther. With each sentence he spat out, I constantly lost focus as the sight of his large fangs sent my anxiety through the roof. I turned to Darius, who had now begun to unthaw. He was soaking wet and shivering on the floor.

"Okay, look, please don't hurt us. What is it that you want? I take it's the Night Script you're after."

Belphegor's face came to a Grinch-like smile as he slowly approached. Terrified with fear, I stepped back, tripping over the glass table behind me. As I plummeted towards an impaling disaster, Belphegor simply wiggled his ears, stopping me mid-fall. Whatever magic he was casting pulled me back to a vertical position, leaving my feet hovering inches from the ground.

"I've heard of said text. And while it possesses many spells that could prove problematic, alas, that is not why I am here. It seems you and I have a common foe, Ms. Graham. "The night Athame, Midworld Pendulum. The great feed of Prana, my brethren Gamigin."

Wait, am I hearing this correctly? This creature is Gamigin's brother! What exactly is going on here? It seems as if things just went from bad to *"Welp, we're doomed."* Alvin was quiet. He could feel the gears in his mind churning. He had questions, a great deal of them.

"Pheebs, if Gamigin is his brother, then why is he willing to help us?"

"Right, good point, let's ask him ... " I shouted aloud.

"So, if Gamigin is your brother, why would you..."

"Help you!" chortled Belphegor.

"Ms. Graham, if your friend has an inquiry, by all means, allow him to take the floor."

A puzzled look became plastered upon my face. It felt as if Belphegor was not only reading my thoughts, but he could sense Alvin's presence as well. But how, how was he doing this?

"You see, Mister Casen, I am in possession of a very unique item. An item that my brother so badly desires, the Volkman's Stone."

Volkman's stone, well, this is a new one for me. I'd like to think I had a good handle on all of the magical artifacts in my life these days, i.e., the *Night Script*, which has been a pain in my side, yet Alvin has never mentioned a Volkmann's Stone.

"My dear Phoebe, the reason your friend has never mentioned the stone is because he would have no knowledge of it," purred Belphegor.

Alvin shrugged his shoulders in agreement, applying a smug smirk to his innocence.

"So, what's the deal with this stupid stone then!" shouted Darius with a shiver in his voice.

"Listen closely, my short-minded human friends, as I am only going to explain this once. After the Hierophant War, the angels took great pleasure in banishing my brethren and me to a realm called Eidolon Plateau. A dreadful place where time seemingly stands still and the floors are lined with molten brimstone. And to make matters worse, a failsafe had been implemented to ensure our escape would never happen... "The Ogun Net."

"We suffered for centuries, that is, until I developed a tool that would allow for a small rip within the net, the Volkman's Stone. You see, my brothers are warriors, brutes if you may. But I, I favor the dark arts. As the stone's creator, I am the only one familiar with its

137

power, or at least I was. Upon making it to the human realm, the angels became privy to the tool in my possession. They knew it would only be a matter of time before I synthesized human cruelty, greed, and desires to boost the stone's abilities, thus freeing my brothers from Eidolon. So, an accord was made, leaning heavily in my favor. You see, the evils of men began to go unchecked. Balance was required, an unlimited feast for my growing appetite. Not to mention an army of minions and, most importantly, immunity and from an angel's blade, all of the world's wicked souls, fresh for my picking. So long as I refused to use the stone to free my brothers, I could hardly pass on such a bargain, I, the Earth's one true Devil. Yet I must admit, I did not foresee Gamigin making it to this world, and make no mistake, he will not only hunt down the stone, but he will try to take my head as well. Yet, I sense my brother is at a disadvantage; he has no physical form, which means no complete power, and with no complete power or Night Script, he can't cast Sempiternal Eye. Which in turn also means finding me is now borderline impossible."

Should have known better. How shocking a devil looking out for himself. Clearly, my trust levels were now inflated, but what choice did we have? I have to get Garrett back, free Louise, and somehow send Gamigin back to wherever he hails from.

Before I could fix my lips to ask the burning question, a ball of light appeared, projecting Alvin's voice, similar to the way he had communicated with Darius.

"What's the deal?" asked Alvin in an aggressive tone.

Darius and I turned our heads toward the glowing orb. Kinda odd to hear Alvin be so stern.

"What, we're all thinking about it. Might as well get on with it. Tell me I'm wrong, Pheebs, Darius, any thoughts?"

Darius and I looked at one another. Yeah, slim pickings was the word of the day. A deal with the Devil it is.

"Splendid, absolutely splendid. Now, onto business. As mentioned before, my brother Gamigin seeks three things: the Night Script, the Volkmans stone, and last but not least, freeing our fellow Devils. But with this, we can put an end to it all."

Belphegor snapped his blade of a claw, revealing a tattered but elegant scroll of sorts, gingerly tied with a purple sash. The scroll possessed an eerie glow with the hum of a lightsaber. Geeky description, but it's the best I got. The three of us couldn't help but marvel at such an object. But how does this help us?

Flicking the text to an unraveling, Belphegor revealed the most beautiful penmanship I had ever laid eyes on. The strange text gave a gold-like shimmer, almost holographic in nature. It's as if the letters hovered and danced above the old papyrus.

"It never gets old," cackled Belphegor.

"Humans, such limited minds, oh so fascinated with a little magic. But I digress. This is the Hekla Leaf. Now you may be wondering, Belphegor, how does this help? Well, tis quite simple, actually. The Hekla Leaf contains the true names of nine Devils. Tis and only tis is your best defense against Gamigin. Utter his true name, and your problems are solved, that simple. Everyone wins. With that, I shall leave thou to it."

After rebinding the Hekla Leaf, the sly cat snapped his claws, summoning a purple vortex, and proceeded to place one furry foot within. Wow, this is actually happening. This is our ticket to victory. I snatched the Hekla Leaf from Belphegor's claws, quickly unraveling it from its sash. Finally, a tool to save Garrett and Louise.

"Phoebe, wait!" shouted Darius.

"There's more here than meets the eye. Nine names, huh? That's cool and all. But we don't know which name is Gamigins. I have a hunch our boy here is leaving details out. Aren't you...Belphegor."

Belphegor stopped in his tracks, quickly pulling back his jet-black slipper of a foot. Turning his head with a twitch of annoyance, Belphegor's cat-like ears pinned back like tiny arrowheads. Oh no, I know that look. My cat Sith does the same thing when he's about to turn my leg into a scratching post.

"Sigh, I can see they are not as dumb as they look. Very well, yes, there are rules to using thy Hekla Leaf. For one, you must be within five feet of Gamigin to speak his name. And as for which one of those names belongs to my dear brother, well, that's for me to know and you to find out."

I knew it. I knew it! This stupid cat is a liar, and of course, there's a catch.

"Okay," I hissed.

"Fine, don't tell us, but I don't get it! First, you say you'll help us, and then you don't. What the heck was the point of it? I swear if I find out which one of these names belongs to you, I'll shout it out without hesitation. And send you back to wherever you came from."

140

Belphegor was clearly ignoring me, and to top it off, he had the audacity to groom himself in the midst of my rant. Guess I was boring him. Man, cats are rude! Look at him just licking his paw, cleaning in tandem with his rumbling purring.

Belphegor proceeded to release a massive yawn.

"Well, good luck with that. Part of my bargain with the Angels was to have my name removed from that list. Hence, nine names as opposed to ten. But you do have a point…human, it would make sense to just tell you my brother's name? However, I am a Devil and a cat. Call it instincts, but I can't resist toying with food. Should you fail, I suppose I'll have to deal with my dearest brother by my lonesome and request the aid of the Angels. And you know how Angels work. They just can't resist a good purge. I'm sure if Gamigin gets too out of hand, they'll just wipe out humankind and start anew. Till then, ta-ta, don't let me down."

Belphegor vanished into the vortex as Darius, Alvin, and I stood in the living room, more confused than ever. I plopped down onto the couch, taking a swig from the warm bottle of Moscato resting on the table. Devils, I tell ya, what a bunch of cutthroats. Can't believe Belphegor is willing to betray his own family for power and food. And to make matters worse, if we fail, the entire human race could be eradicated by Angels. No, I won't let that happen. With that being said, I lifted the Hekla Leaf, analyzing it from top to bottom. The good news was that all of the text, besides the names, seemed to be written in Latin. What a shocker. Angels and Devils love their Latin. But the mystery remains: which one of these names was Gamigins? Darius took a seat on the couch next to me and began scouring the Hekla Leaf as well.

"I don't know, Pheebs. Maybe we'll get lucky. What if his name is the first on the list?"

"What if it's the last?" Alvin added.

"Fair points to both of them. Nine names: Hum...Dinileth, Pharzuph, Glasya-labolas, Kunops, Epinon, Halpas, Abaddon, Xaphan, and Egyn, none short of a mouthful to say. Alvin, I think we have to go with Darius on this one. We're out of time. I say we follow the Draad trail right into the belly of the beast. We know it's a trap, so we just get out in front of it."

Alvin's emotions began to sparkle. This wasn't anger or disappointment with my decision. This was excitement. I could feel it in Alvin's bones. He wanted revenge for his mother and atonement for himself.

"Welp, enough talk, lovebirds. Let's do it!"

In my mind's eye, I was able to see Alvin removing his blazer and rolling up the sleeves of his crisp white shirt like some overworked detective.

"Darius, you up for this?"

Darius' fingers slowly tinkled towards mine, like cords on a grand piano. He grabbed the tips of my fingers, rubbing them gently.

"For this girl, Alvin...I'd do anything."

The next few hours, we tweaked our bum-rush plan. It was fairly simple in theory: A, follow the Draad trail and ensure that Garrett is okay; B, once this is confirmed, we bargain with the Night Script for his release; or C, with Garrett now safe and sound, Darius will cause a mild distract that ion in Louise's direction. That's when I'll start rambling off the names, crossing my fingers, hoping Gamigin's name is one of the first two. As for the Hekla Leaf, well, we can't just tap dance in trying to use it extemporaneously. I'm willing to bet Gamigin's magic works fast, and if he so much as catches a glimpse of the Hekla Leaf, it's game over. Timing will be everything, so Alvin cooked up a nifty minor spell that would not only conceal the scroll but allow it to hover right in front of my face for easy reading.

Gotta say it was pretty ingenious. It felt as if this plan was now bulletproof, but someone please tell that to my gut. I sprang from the couch, dashing to the bathroom sink, refunding any food my stomach was harboring. Turning the faucet handles hot water to the max. I lifted my head to the now foggy mirror. Sliding my sleeve towards the lines in my palm, I swiped away the steam, revealing Alvin's reflection.

"Back where it all began, huh," shrugged Alvin.

"Funny how that works, right? Hey, look, Pheebs, there's a chance that one of us doesn't make it back. But just in case, I want to say my time with you has been more important to me than all of the lifetimes that I have lived. I wouldn't trade our time for the world. We're a good team, you and I. You're a great, strong person and an amazing friend."

Alvin's kind words pulled on my heartstrings. I knew he meant every word, even the part about one of us not making it back. I started to question my own choices. Was I being selfish by pulling Darius into this madness? How could I ever forgive myself if something happened to him? And worst of all, it would crush his mother's fragile heart.

143

Giving Alvin an unsure nod of approval, I made my way back to my living room to break the news to Darius. I've made my decision.

"Darius, can we talk for a second?"

Darius jumped to his feet, his imposing physique towering over my miniature frame like a Jenga tower to an insect. He's not going to like what I'm going to say, but…

"Nope, not happening," Darius riposted.

"I figured this was coming, Pheebs, and before it blows out of proportion, let me just get this off my chest. I care about you a lot. More than I've ever had for anyone. And I know I shouldn't say this, but who knows where this road is going to take us. Phoebe, umm… I love you. And there is no way I'm letting you get at this alone."

I was frozen, stuck in the moment like a tiny dancer in a jewelry box. He said he… loves me. My heart was melting like ice on a salted sidewalk. I was overcome with emotions, my mind disconnected from my lips as I hugged his waist tightly. I was in heaven as Darius' arms wrapped around me with the squeeze of a gentle python.

"I love you, too."

Darius placed his hands upon my blushing rouge cheeks, sneaking in a kiss as soft as lamb's wool.

"We're a team, okay. Where you go, I go, Pheebs."

That settles it. Guess I'm not changing any minds here. Time to head out. Darius, Alvin, and I made our way outside, grabbing the Night Script as our bargaining chip. As I closed my apartment door, I couldn't help but feel as if a new chapter was in the works. Three strangers were now thrust into the

144

universe of danger, adventures, and constant uncertainties. They were not the first humans to deal with the Devil and certainly not the last. These creatures will always rise from the dirt, weeds choking out humanity in pursuit of their own desires. I could see the Draad trail leading the way to my fate. Welp, if this devil wants me, he's going to have to catch me first.

The Draad trail was a strange one, twisting and turning like a recalculating GPS. Gosh, I hope Garrett is okay, and how on earth did Louise get him this far? The three of us bounced around Manhattan like a dive bar pinball. East 4th Street to East 9th Street, East 9th Street to East 14th, East 14th all the way up to East 24th, then back to 5th Ave. I was starting to get flustered. Where on earth was this stupid thing taking us?

"I don't know, Pheebs, this Draad trail seems to be pointless," echoed Alvin's voice.

"I mean, surely we would have found it by…now."

There it was, the end of the Draad trail, our destination, The Flatiron Building. Leave it to a devil to live in style.

"Al, time to cast that spell you cooked up to hide the Hekla Leaf."

Alvin's spell whisked and whipped around my body, coming to a glamorous halt before my eyes. It was like having a VR headset as the Hekla Leaf moved in the exact direction of my pupils. With the spell in full effect, our grand trio entered the famous structure without any knowledge of where to look next. However, before we could begin our investigation, a concierge approached.

"Miss Graham, my master awaits your arrival."

The concierge's eyes, I'd recognize those eyes anywhere! They had an enigmatic glow, very similar to the waiter's eyes at the coffee shop during my first date with Darius.

"The Tertius oculus!" I loudly whispered before clapping my sweaty hands over my mouth.

That was a spell used to control minds. Gamigin's power must be next level. When I used that spell, I was limited to about 30 seconds. This guy seems to be under his control permanently. Making matters worse, it's not just the concierge. It's everyone in the building. As we approached the main lobby, the zombified employees surrounded us on both sides, leaving only a line of sight to the main elevator.

I felt as if Gamigin had updated the menu, and we were now the main course. Some of the now zombified employees sported large fangs, even horns and nails protruding to a point.

"Pheebs, I hope these guys don't decide to lose their cool. We are severely outnumbered," bemoaned Alvin. *"Gamigin is strong. For him to proselyte so many souls so fast is unreal."*

Darius grabbed my waist, pulling me close as we waded through the marsh of glowing eyes.

"Look at these poor people, Pheebs. They have no idea what's happening to them. This is horrible. Do you think Garrett is…"

"We can't think like that, Darius. We just have to press on, stick to our guns, and get Garrett out of here."

As we inched closer to the elevator, the antique position dial above slowly arched to floor one. With a forceful woosh, the bronze-colored doors rattled open, revealing a very confident-looking Louise. Okay, this is just getting out of hand. She looks more glamorous than before. Louise was draped from head to toe. She wore an amazing high-slit cheongsam dress with her Chun-Li-like thighs exposed. Festooned across her shoulders rested a black blazer bolstering massive golden epaulets seemingly not of this world. Louise resembled something more of the likes of a general than a mere servant to Gamigin. Her eye color was now a lambent viridity and a small set of scurs protruded from her long, ink-colored hair.

"Glad to see you were able to make it, Phoebe. And look, you even brought your boy toy and ghost friend with you. How cute."

Louise's power must be intensifying as well, as she's capable of sensing Alvin's presence now.

"Enough with the insults, Louise. Is Garrett okay, and where is he?"

"Pushy, pushy, aren't we? Don't worry your daddy is just fine. But I won't be able to say the same for you and your friends if you don't have my master's Night Script."

"Garrett first, then it's all yours," I bargained.

"Let me see it! My master is not one for games or wasted time," gnashed Louise, exhibiting her now fang-like canines.

Reaching into the bag I was carrying, I revealed the Night Script and all its fame. To think all of this started due to this dusty old book.

"Here you go, take your stupid book, now give me Garrett."

Louise burst into a feverish laugh.

"Oh no, boo. It doesn't work like that. You will kneel, like the petty-bourgeois that you are, and gift the Night Script to The Mighty Night Athame. You three should be

happy. At least you'll have the chance to bask in his glory. Even if it is, as ya know… unworthy."

I've had it with her! I was hitting my boiling point, and my temper was begging to get the best of me. I could even feel that unsightly vein that I get on my forehead when I'm angry. One thing about me, though, is that I may not be the toughest wrench in the toolbox, but I can talk some smack.

"Petty bourgeois, huh? Did your new Devil Sugar Daddy teach you that word? I mean, he's a bit old for my liking, but ya know what they say… 'age ain't nothing but a number,' I guess."

"Umm, Pheebs probably not the best idea," whispered Alvin.

With blistering speed, Louise teleported. Before any of us could so much as bat an eyelash, her red polished claws had an unyielding grip upon my throat. Louise bashed my skull into the corner of the elevator car. Darius sprang into action only to be warned of obtrusion.

"Don't even try it…Darius! If you so much as breathe funny, I will rip your little girlfriend's throat open."

"Easy, Darius, not here," hummed Alvin's voice.

"Good, glad to see we are all on the same…page. Get it, page!" Louise broke into uproarious laughter.

"Here we are, kiddo's lucky 22. Let's move out."

Exiting the elevator, the three of us followed Louise's strut down a sequence of candle-lit halls. Evil was permeating through each hall. The closer the proximity, the more forlorn I began to feel. After about a minute's stroll, we finally reached what felt to be Gamigin's domain. Louise reached into her blazer, divulging an antique Barrel Key. Smirking in my direction, Louise pressed her pouty vermilion lips together to a mwah, followed by a wink. I could feel Alvin's blood pressure rising. His throat was dying out, as was my own. I looked over to Darius, gripping his hand tightly, looking deep into his eyes as if it may be our last. This was it. Time to put up or shut up. As she twisted the key, pushing forward the bulky door, the once luxury apartment now resembled something just shy of Pharaoh's throne room. Gold had now encased the structure. Witch-like sigils had been carved into every support beam. This room was pure evil. In the center of the room were two gold statues in the form of foxes nestled in between the two idols, a monumental-sized throne embracing an unconscious Garrett. My emotions were getting the better of me as he was showing clear signs of life.

"Garrett!" I shouted. My screams and pain were clear as they reverberated throughout the room.

"Quiet, he's perfectly fine. Now kneel," demanded Louise!

"Master Gamigin, your guests have arrived. At long last."

Stepping from behind the great throne, a massive figure appeared. It was Gamigin. His physique was titanic, muscular in build, and standing at the height of ten feet or greater. His skin was the color of bronze, with a flourish of golden fur surfing towards his neck. Gamigin's head was that of a fox, his eyes a deep, hypnotizing gold. To top off the fear, Gamigin flexed his back, jetting out a giant set of bat wings. Darius appeared to be in a state of disbelief, as did Alvin. Gamigin's lips did not move, but his sonorous voice could be heard ripping through the room.

"So, you are the one who wields my Night Script. Louise has provided much insight into your world, Miss Graham. I'm sure I require no formal introduction."

Chapter Ten
The Kaleidoscope

Remember that bum-rush plan we had in the works? Well, that went out the window faster than expected. Gamigin stepped down from the sunken platform bearing his throne. I could feel each thump of his massive feet galloping toward us. Fear couldn't describe the feeling within my core, but as Gamigin approached, it seemed as if he were more elegant than initially presumed. Slowing his stride, Gamigin paused as he seemingly studied Dauris and me.

"Interesting. I have met many humans in my lifetime, but you, Miss Graham, seem to be the only one withholding a secondary soul. Alvin, is it?"

Gamigin circled the three of us like a wild dog seeking his next meal. I could tell Darius wanted to react, but it was evident that it would be suicide. Dissipating before our eyes, appearing like a ghost behind me, Gamigin forced the hairs on my neck to about-face, resting his massing paws upon my shoulders like a proud father in a family photo.

"You know Phoebe, my beautiful Louise has shown me a lot since joining my sect. You and I share many likenesses."

I knew this was my chance. I had more than enough range to use the Halka Leaf, but maybe too close. If I rambled off the wrong name, this guy was going to rip me in half. I had to stall.

"Humans and Devils: alike? What brought you to that crazy conclusion?"

Snapping his claws, everyone in the golden room appeared in a fancy dining hall. The table we were seated at extended at least seven feet with Gamigin at the head. Drat, out of range.

"Maybe he's onto us. Who just up and creates a Refectory table? He's keeping his distance now," whispered Alvin.

Alvin had a point, but nothing we could do now. Such a regal banquet. What was he playing at? Roasted boar, cornucopias of fruits and cheeses, along with various meats, garnished the table. Gamigin himself even changed a bit. He was now wearing what I would describe as Egyptian-style armor. Taking a brief sip of the gaudy goblet in front of him, Gamigin began to speak again.

"Do you fear me, child?"

I was perplexed. Was this some sort of test? He's trying to see if I'm just another pushover.

"Cut the head games. I have your Night Script. Now give me Garrett."

"I have seen your world in its infancy, and now I see it in its prime. Like Devils, humans often fight for the greater good of their species. But also have a tendency to let your greed interfere with progress. You crave the idea of power, presenting the ideology of Alpha and Omega. I have seen women and children beaten by men and men beaten by their possessor, whether it be with a whip or by law. Savages salivating at the pallet of another's woes."

Gamigin was trying to poke around in my mind. Opening and closing each bank like a refrigerator during a midnight snack. What was he looking for?

"Even now, as we speak, you know what I wish to accomplish with the Night Script. Yet, all you speak of is freeing your role model. You do not care what I do as long as your plans go unchallenged. You feel it, Miss Graham. Don't you? That selfish inkling that's very Devil of you, is it not?"

"You don't know anything about her," exclaimed Darius, slamming his fist into the oak!

Gamigin raised his paw, bringing his serrated claws to a tight seal. A heavy aura came crashing into the room, forcing Darius back into his seat. The pressure was immense. Darius looked as if he were being slowly crushed. Vaulting to my feet, I began to plead for the torture to cease.

"Enough! Why are you doing this? I have your Night Script; just take it and leave us be."

Gamigin and Louise both began to hoot with laughter. Did I miss the joke or something?

"While yes, you are indeed correct, it is 'my Night Script,' and to answer your question as to why, well, it's simple. I want you to break! You see, Miss Graham, you are going to be my example, a statement piece, if you will. I will crush your spirit, over and over and over, until you give in to your inner evils. You will be the poster child, proof to the angels that all humans are nothing but selfish food. There is no such thing as a 'good human.' With our numbers, we are no match for the Angels, yet with proof, they will see that all along, they have been protecting an apocryphal belief. With that vision, my legion will be

granted full reign upon the human world, with an endless food supply."

This was sick. How could this psycho ever think that all humans are all wicked? It was pure ignorance, and I refused to let my own doubt get the best of me. For too long, I have given people who have no leading role in the movie of my life the ability to play the director. This is my moment, and these are my choices.

"You're wrong, Gamigin. Humans aren't just wicked food, and yeah, we do have a few bad apples in the bunch, but you can't lump us all together. I won't let you."

Pushing back his elegant chair, Gamigin soared to his feet. The hulking Fox proceeded to lift his goblet once more, taking a massive lap before locking me into a stare-down. Picking up the Night Script, I swiped the tattered book's texture with my thumbs. What a wild ride it's been.

"And here I thought I was being generous, Miss Graham. This was supposed to be your last supper. What a pity."

It seemed Gamigin's hold on Darius had released itself. The once chic dining hall had disappeared as we were now back in the throne room. Taking a deep breath, I glanced in Darius' direction. He knew exactly what I was thinking.

"If you want this Night Script, you're going to have to take it," I barbed.

Alvin's voice was looping in my inner ear. I take it he was not pleased with my enkindling of Gamigin's wrath. Enough waiting. Gamigin, slow in his pace, began to approach. My mind was trying my best to gauge the distance of his stride. It was now or never. I studied the Halka Leaf as time began to feel sedated. Looking in the direction of the throne, I noticed Garrett was coming to his senses. Taking one last gulp, I spat out the first name on the list.

"Dinileth!"

Gamigin came to a gruff stop. The look on his face was one of total shock and confusion. Had he been bested by a simple human once again? Was I so lucky as to get his true name correct on the first breath? As an avid comic book reader, I should have known that was wishful thinking. Nothing was happening, and before I could fix my lips to launch the next name, Gamigin stretched out his cosmic arm, gesturing my body into the air like a paper kite. Amidst my screaming, I offered my best attempt at speaking the second name on the list.

Gamigin's magic was fast. He quickly cast a spell, slapping a tape-like substance across my mouth. I could feel Alvin inside my mind rambling off a counterspell of sorts. Things seemed to be falling apart at warp speed.

Out of the corner of my eye, I spotted an object of sorts being hurled at Gamigin. It was Darius, and he was angry. I tried to shout for him to stay back, but it was no use. He was on a warpath. Removing his jacket, Darius charged toward Gamigin full steam, only to be caught off guard by a cheap shot of magic from Louise.

"Get up!" Sneered Louise as she unleashed a furry of magic blows upon Darius.

Tattered and sizzling, Darius refused to concede even as she towered above his beaten body.

Like any good sadist, Gamigin licked his snout at the sight of Darius' agony as he proceeded to question my knowledge of the name I had spoken.

"Miss Graham, you are indeed full of many surprises, yet that name predates you by several thousands of years. While I do not doubt your ingenuity, I have my doubts regarding your knack for stumbling upon Mephistophelian items."

Cutting Gamigin's monologue short, Darius found the will and strength to rise to his feet and tackle Louise, knocking over various objects in the process. Infuriated, Louise launched a stiff beam of magic toward Darius. As I watched in horror, it seemed as if Alvin's prediction would come to pass. One of us was going to die.

"Darius, block it. Grab the glass platter and block it," it was Alvin. I totally forgot that he and Darius could communicate.

"Get the platter you knocked over!"

With the haste of a frightened squirrel, Darius quickly scurried to the glass platter behind him, flipping the lavish item to its reflective side in Louise's direction. The bright beam clashed with the glass surface like a high school science project. It was a direct hit. Louise's own magic sent her flying like a homerun baseball in Yankee Stadium! Was she...dead?

Snapping his concentration, Gamigin released an unmelodious roar, expanding his wings and bursting into Louise's direction. Who would have guessed that a devil like Gamigin has a soft spot for an actual human? Gotta save the psychoanalysis for later. My chance to end this nonsense was back in full effect.

"Look what you've done, you filthy grubs! My Louise, my sweet Louise. You will burn for this," screamed Gamigin!

He was rabid. Drool was foaming from his muzzle as he exhibited his blade-like teeth. Do or die time! Without thinking, I sprinted in Gamigin's direction, studying the pronunciation of the next name.

"Pharzuph!"

"Wrong again. Wrong, wrong!"

Gamigin lifted his bruiser of a claw once more, aiming it in my direction and sending the rubber soles of my Nike shoes to a sliding stop. Electricity was popping and sizzling from his palm as he released a misty green ray of light. The odd lifelike beam lifted Garrett to the height of the rafters, encasing him within an oozing substance, and sent him into a blood-chilling scream.

"One more feed," smiled the devilish Gamigin, licking his chops!

"The beauty is that I misjudged. I don't require this meal, but I shall truly enjoy it!"

"I'm far beyond complete, but this one is for my Louise! An eye for an eye, a tooth for a tooth, a love for a love."

Watching in horror, Darius, Alvin, and I couldn't believe the power we were witnessing. It seemed Garrett had been drained of all life. Tossing Garrett's now lifeless body to the ground before my very feet, I was in a total state of aghast. My soul, my entire world, had just been crushed like a cookie in the hand of a toddler. Garrett was not just a friend. He was the father I've always needed. He was a gentle soul who gave me a chance when no one else believed in me.

Falling to my knees, I hugged the Night Script, hoping some sort of magic would come from my tears as they dropped upon the tattered text. There's that little girl in me again, hoping that, just for once, a fairy tale would come true. Darius, beaten and bruised, staggered to my side, realizing that he was probably next on the chopping block.

"Phoebe, Phoebe," shouted Alvin, trying to snap me out of my current state ajar!

"Phoebe, get up. You have to move. He's coming this way. Phoebe, please get up!"

Alvin's words were no good. I was lost. I was defeated.

"Al, I don't care what he does to me at this point. I'm finished."

As I prepared to roll over and accept not only my fate but the fate of all mankind. The beast known as Gamigin inched closer and closer to me like a dark cloud, yet keeping just enough distance in case I knew of any other names. Figuring these would be the last words the world would hear from me, I removed my cracked phone from my tattered jeans pocket and began recording my goodbyes.

But these goodbyes weren't for me. They were for Gamigin. Quickly pressing play on my mobile recording, I slid the phone across the smooth gold floor like a game of Air Hockey, right in Gamigin's direction. The wavelengths from my phone recording danced across the glass screen like an EKG.

"Glasya-labolas, Kunops, Epinon, Halpas, Abaddon, Xaphan, and Egyn!"

All of the remaining names over and over again. I was not sure which one was Gamigin's, but it didn't matter. That phone was well in range to put an end to this creep.

Darius, Alvin, and I watched in stupefaction as a bright white light burst through the solid gold floor. A raging whirlwind whipped within the corridors of the Flatiron, seemingly sucking in all that was evil. Gamigin, the once powerful Night Athame, Midworld Pendulum, clawed at the floor like a dog searching for a buried bone. The powers of the vortex proved to be all too dynamic, pulling the Devil down like an insect stuck in a bathtub drain. Cursing my name in his exit, Gamigin was no more. The once golden room slowly reverted back to its chic Manhattan size and standards. Even the evil that was planted within Louise seemed to vanish. Gone were the scurs that once protruded through her dark mane, unconscious but alive. The same couldn't be said for Garrett.

Lifting his head and placing it gently on my lap, I rested my clammy hand upon his flatlined heart.

"Pheebs, I'm sorry," whispered Darius.

"He was a good man. I'm sure he knows you did everything in your power to save him."

I had no strength to reply to the kind words. The only thing running through my mind was all the good times Garrett and I shared. My once great mentor, guiding light, and father was no more. My mind just couldn't comprehend it.

"I have an idea, Pheebs," sighed Alvin with a melancholy quiver in his tone.

"I can't guarantee anything, but maybe, just maybe, I can bring him back."

"Bring him back?" I questioned with elation.

"How? Never mind that. Please, Alvin, please try! Oh my God, Alvin, you're amazing! If you had a body, I would give you the biggest hug on the planet."

"Wait, you can do that?" questioned Darius.

Alvin went silent; for someone spewing news this good, he sure seemed gloomy. I know Alvin well enough to know when his emotions are running high, yet I couldn't pinpoint what exactly Al was feeling. Was this nervousness, fear, or something more?

"Phoebe, listen closely. I can bring Garrett back the same way I brought you back. However, there are rules."

Taking a gasp of air, I gently stood up from Garrett's now cool body.

"Rules? No, no, no, don't say it! Please don't, Al. I know what 'rules' is slang for, and from my experiences, when someone says rules the way you just did, it's probably a bad thing."

"Phoebe, please just let me finish. Giving my essence to Garrett will bring him back. However, Melding Magic comes with a price. If used more than once, the donor will cease to exist. Magic is a dangerous tool and solely based on give and take."

"Alvin, no, I won't let you!"

"Pheebs, I've made up my mind. I have lived a long life, a good life, and a great life, thanks to you. Just know that wherever I go, I will never ever forget you. You've shown me joy, a joy so great that words don't do it justice. Right now, Garrett needs that same joy. Besides, I'm tired, Pheebs. I think it's time for me to rest... Hey, Darius, you got a good one on your hands. Take care of her, okay."

Just like that, I could see Alvin clearer than I had been able to in a long time. The two of us were standing alone inside an empty subway car. He had Twix-colored hair and deep brown eyes accompanied by the high-end fashion taste of many other New Yorkers in the SOHO area, not to mention he was wearing those stupid 1,000-dollar loafers. As the fictitious train screeched through the tunnel of my mind, Alvin approached.

"Hey, Pheebs, how about that hug?"

As I wrapped my arms around Alvin, my body in the real world began to feel warm. My skin was coming to a tingle akin to the feeling of a foot falling asleep. Looking down at my hands, they began to glow to the point of transparency. The power of the magic became hot, snapping my hair tie and lifting my hair to a bright blonde flame. With one last burst of atoms, the room lit to the brightness of an exploding star. Blinded by the intensity of the light, Darius and I called out to one another like two strangers lost in the woods. As the light began to withdraw, nothing could prepare me for what I would see next. It was Garrett!

"Hey, Kiddo," said Garrett, giving his classic dad thumbs up!

Dashing to his arms, I gave Garrett the biggest hug. It was really him! Alvin did it! Giving him the tightest of squeezes, I was in awe of Garrett's bushy gray beard and narrator-esque voice. I truly thought I'd lost him. Alas, the moment seemed bittersweet. As no clever whips of humor or banter came into my mind, Alvin was truly gone. I was positive Alvin said I needed him to stay alive all those weeks back, but I guess that was another one of his secrets. Me saying I missed him already didn't do my conflicted heart any justice. I wish to keep everyone important to my life here with me. As I looked over Garrett's shoulder, there lay the Night Script covered in a thin layer of dust. Many thoughts ran through my mind. Maybe in some strange, twisted way, Gamigin had a point. Maybe I am selfish, as I quickly scoop up the text before departure.

Darius made his way over to a recovering Louise, extending his arm in assistance. Draping her over his broad shoulder, the four of us made our way to the main lobby of the Flatiron. It appeared everyone had returned to normal. No claws or glowing eyes, just good old-fashioned hustle and bustle. What a night that was!

As the weeks passed, life returned to a strange norm. Garrett had officially moved into his new role with the UK-based publisher. His going away party was a stark reminder of all of the good the world would be missing without him. Louise decided to move on from Monarch, which was totally understandable. As for me, life was good. Darius and I had a blossoming relationship. We even started the move-in together conversation. Like many nights before, I rode the local D train back to my cozy little nook in Midtown. The only problem was that my mind was always too quiet. I had lost my best friend and wasn't sure how to cope.

That night, I sat in my bathroom looking at the Night Script, wondering if a spell existed to bring Al back. I know magic is finicky and solely based on give and take. The question is, what would I have to give? Later that night, as Darius slept, I roamed my apartment, and the idea of some sort of spell danced in my mind like sugar plum fairies. The temptation was real. I could feel the beating pulse of the Night Script. It called out to me with promises and plans. I had to admit the odd book made a convincing case. Holding the Night Script in my palms, I stroked the rusty buckles of the text like Gollum with the ring.

"No, I can't! Alvin wouldn't want this." Throwing the book to the floor, I wrapped it in a dish towel.

This book is my burden, my curse, and my promise to Alvin. I won't use its contents. I will act as its protector to keep it out of the wrong hands. The next morning, I made my way to Monarch. It was back to business. My mind was clear. I sucked up the nonsense like a big girl, worked on another celebrity's stupid book, and even built a better relationship with Amber Lynn as I waited my turn. Little did I know, it wouldn't be that long of a wait as my phone began to ring, flashing Garrett's name.

"Hey Garrett, how goes it? Lunch, sure thing. Cool beans. Sounds like a plan."

"Click."

As the clock struck noon, I met Garrett in a cute little coffee shop nearby for a mild lunch.

"So, Mr. Big Time, how is the new position going? Are you adjusting well to the UK?"

"Amazing, absolutely amazing, London is a dream. I'm so glad we had a chance to grab lunch, kiddo. But let me cut to the chase. Phoebe, it's time. I want you to join my publishing house. My superiors have given me full reign, and as promised, you are going to

be my feature breakout author. I know your work and your talent is extraordinary. So, here's the proposition. You'll have full creative control and a full selection of editors and artists. Then, to top it off, we'll cover your moving expenses. I really talked you up, kid. So, what do you say, are you in? It's the opportunity of a lifetime."

In true basic white girl fashion, I clapped my hands over my mouth and burst into tears. The moment seemed so surreal. With everything that had happened, I couldn't believe Garrett's words, not to mention how well he had recovered. My chance was finally here, my Carrie Bradshaw of a moment. So why was I so hesitant? I think my answer was clear: it was Darius. I was in love with him and couldn't possibly part from him. Not to mention his mother; he takes care of her, and it wouldn't seem fair to pull him away.

"Well, Garrett, the idea is literally a dream come true. But Darius and I have built a life; he is his mother's caretaker, and I'm not sure I should take him away from that so suddenly. You know I want this more than anything. It's just…"

Using his index, Garrett pushed his mate's black frames back to his brow before taking a sip of his soda.

"Of course, kiddo. I totally understand. Look, I'm here until Friday. Tell ya what, talk it over with Darius, and we can go from there. Either way, I'm happy for you. Phoebe, ya know, when my daughter passed, I felt lost, like I was simply living to live. Just a warm body moving through time, day after day. Then everything happened with Louise and that awful

Monster. Phoebe, you really put your neck out there for me, and I'll never forget it. You've given me that spark back, kid. You showed me that I've still got a lot to live for, as well as people who really care about me. Guess what I'm trying to say is thank you for everything."

After finishing our swanky lunch, I carved out another successful day at Monarch. As I traveled back to my apartment, I couldn't help but think of the fresh start this opportunity would provide. However, only trick coins have the same side, the other being my life with Darius. As I turned the key to my flat, a sweet aroma was wafting through the crack of my door. I walked in to find Darius cooking up an amazing meal: tacos, of course, our favorite. It was now or never. I had to pick his brain. Time to poke the elephant in the room with a stick.

"Hey, Pheebs, how was the office?"

"Good, actually great. Well, as great as it can be, ha."

God, could I sound any more dorkish? What does this man see in me?

"So, hey, D. Garrett is in town. We met for lunch."

"Oh dope," nodded Darius, typical Mr. Cool.

"He seems to be holding up well, considering everything that has happened. He's happy with the UK position... And he actually asked me to join his house as a feature author."

It was becoming harder and harder to read Darius. Even his cooking pace slowed as the spatula mashed and smashed far less into the bubbling ground beef. Clearing his throat, he finally responded.

"Wow, oh wow, that's awesome babe! So, are you going to do it?" replied Darius, chomping on a Pico-filled tortilla chip.

I wasn't exactly sure how to respond. It was definitely a dream, but so was Darius. I guess this is how life goes. Every decision can shape your future. We're a team, and nothing can break that, not even dreams or nightmares.

"If I'm honest, my heart wants to, but not if it doesn't include you."

Licking the salsa from his thumb, Darius released a chuckle before planting a kiss on my cold lips.

"Do it. I would never keep you from your dreams, Pheebs. We'll figure it out. Heck, I'll go with you!"

My heart started to flutter with excitement. He really is a standup guy. How did I ever find him? I guess if it weren't for Alvin, none of this would be happening. I just wish he was around to be a part of it.

"What about your mother? Who is going to take care of her?"

Taking a deep breath, suggesting that it was a bridge he had not yet crossed, our excitement got the better of us and forced a surprise visit to Darius' mother in Queens. Talk about being the sweetest, Darius' mother suggested that he go, not ever wanting to hold him back from something he believed would better himself. Even his aunt gave two cents, stating she would take good care of her sister in his absence. They really were a tight-knit family. This much is true: should Darius and I take our relationship to the next level one day, it's safe to say I'm in good hands. I couldn't thank them enough for allowing us to chase our dreams. So, it was settled, London it is.

166

I phoned Garrett, setting up dinner to tell him the good news in person. As the three of us celebrated toasting and laughing at new beginnings, I spotted Louise across the street through the restaurant's glaring bay window. She looked good, even retaining a bit of the glamour influence left by Gamigin. Pushing my seat back to a screech, I sprinted away from my meal to greet her.

"Louise, hey, it's Phoebe!"

It was great to see Louise back to herself, but she still was missing something. It was as if she was lost. I guess none of us will know the real toll Gamigin took on her or how deep his talons ripped into her soul. Even so, that doesn't mean we can't be friends. Placing my chilly hands in my pockets, I pushed for small talk.

"So, girl, how have you been holding up? How's life away from Monarch?"

"Yeah, it's good. I just had to get away from that place. Too many bad memories, ya know. Besides I think the lit world isn't as much of my thing as I thought it would be. How about you? Everything seems to be going well with you guys." Pointing to Darius and Garrett, chatting it up in the window.

"Yeah, everything is good." I wasn't really sure what to say, as I didn't want to seem as if I was rubbing her nose into my life.

"Heard you're off to Jolly ol London." Smiled Louise, blowing her cig smoke into the frosty air.

"Yeah, um, I took a position with Garrett. So, Dauris and I are going to take the plunge. I mean, ya only live once, right? We fly out next week."

167

"Wow, good for you guys," she said, throwing her cig to the ground, mashing it with the tip of her Doc Martens. Yet, my intuition was telling me Louise had more on her mind.

"Hey, Pheebs, this may seem totally random, and you can totally say no. But...would you mind if I tagged along? Just until London, then I'll be on my way. I can get my own ticket and all. I just figured, why not travel with friends for a bit? Then, once we land, I'll be out of your hair. Then it's off to Paris for me."

Lighting up another cig, Louise stroked the dark, wispy hair from her eyes.

"Hey, Pheebs, can I tell you something? And promise not to judge. Is it wrong that I kinda miss him? Ya know, Gamigin. It's just that we bonded. I know what he was, but he loved me. Am I crazy?"

I can't say that I blame her. Gamigin had complete control of her for over a month. And unlike my situation with Alvin, she had no knowledge or say-so of anything. After something that traumatic, you probably require years of recovery.

"No, you're not crazy. I mean, I fell for Alvin at one point. Some bonds transcend our idea of good and bad."

Louise flicked her cig, brandishing a smile of relief. I'm glad we had this talk. Louise and I aren't so different after all. Looking up at New York's night sky, I couldn't help but add one more splash of my cheesy humor.

"So, Paris eh, Ooh la la."

The next few days were full of hustle and rush, packing, closeouts, and long goodbyes. Amber Lynn

168

rolled out the red carpet for my departure while Chris groveled over my younger replacement. As the four pressed on, scrambling like mice through the twists and turns of JFK, we eventually landed in Heathrow. This is where we said our final goodbyes to Louise. *"To Paris, Rome then who knows was her slogan."* Garrett offered her room and board along with a job, but sometimes, one's own steam is best. As for Darius and I, we managed to find a small little flat in the Covent Garden area of London. Darius even rekindled his love of technology and even made a friend, some nerdy guy named Tyler Pine. But what the heck? He was able to land Darius a pretty sweet gig.

As for me, it was time to start my first book, which is about a girl who gets possessed and slays a devil. A bit on the nose, sure, why not?

"Pheebs, I'm home. How's the writing going? Have you come up with a title for your book yet?"

"Yeah, how's this one? *'The Devil Catches Butterflies.'"*

The End

About the Author

New York-based author Reese T. Lightfoot is a versatile wordsmith who weaves tales that dazzle the imagination. Reese plunges his readers into a world of Fantasy blended with modern-day pop culture. With a penchant for exploring the nuances of Geekdom, Reese's storytelling invites readers into rich tapestries of heroes and villains, monsters and magic teetering the fault lines of his vivid imagination. His literary journey is marked by a desire to craft narratives that resonate with his audience while staying true to his passions for anime, manga, film, and comic books. Most at home navigating the ever-expanding waters of fiction, Reese's work is a true testament to embracing one's inner desires and traversing the landscape of his own inventiveness. Every page written is an uncharted journey. The question is, are you adventurous enough to tag along?

Printed in the USA
CPSIA information can be obtained
at www.ICGtesting.com
LVHW040526170324
774566LV00001B/190